DOUBLE TAKE

by
L. D. Tetlow

Dales Large Print Books
Long Preston, North Yorkshire,
England.

British Library Cataloguing in Publication Data.

Tetlow, L.D.
    Double take.

A catalogue record for this book is
available from the British Library

ISBN 1-85389-971-2

First published in Great Britain by Robert Hale Ltd., 1998

Published in Large Print 1999 by arrangement with Robert
Hale Ltd.

Dales Large Print is an imprint of
Library Magna Books Ltd.
Printed and bound in Great Britain by
T.J. International Ltd., Cornwall, PL28 8RW.

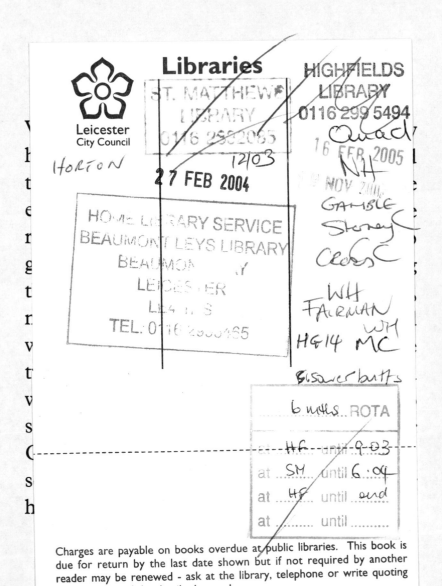

ONE

Had Caleb been travelling just that little bit faster, or had the bullet been that fraction of an inch further to the left, there would have been no doubt that it would have been Caleb's head which was shattered and not the bark of the tree he happened to be passing. His immediate reaction was dictated by the pure instinct of survival in that he tumbled from his horse and played dead, but at the same time he drew one of his two Colt pistols and ensured that he landed in such a position so as to hide the weapon but have it ready for use. He hit the ground a little heavier than he had intended, jarring his shoulder, but he ignored this minor discomfort and waited for whomsoever had shot at him to show themselves as he knew they must. They would be unable to resist gloating and checking on the accuracy of their shot and he did not have too long to wait.

'You must've killed him,' came a rather juvenile-sounding voice. 'Man, that was sure some fancy shootin'.'

'Told you I could,' said another juvenile voice. 'I been puttin' in a lot of practice lately. Anyhow, that's one bastard less; all we got to do now is find the others.'

The two youths came closer to the body and, although they appeared quite convinced that their target was dead, they seemed a little apprehensive and at first they viewed the body from a safe distance and were partly hidden by a tree. When, after about a minute, there was no movement, they crept a little closer.

'Don't see no blood,' said the first juvenile voice. 'There should be blood, lots of it, or at least his brains should be runnin' out, just like when Pa shot our old dog with the shotgun.' Caleb thought that he sounded quite disappointed. 'I guess that was a shotgun though, they allus make more mess than a rifle,' he added.

'Maybe blacks don't have no blood or brains,' said the second voice. 'Pa allus reckoned they was different from whites.' They moved even closer and bent down to examine their kill only to find themselves staring into the barrel of Caleb's Colt. Neither youth uttered a sound and seemed totally incapable of moving, the rifle in the second youth's hand falling from his grasp.

'Then your pa was wrong,' grinned Caleb. 'I can assure you us blacks have just as much blood as you whites an' it's the same colour. Not only that but our shit stinks just the same as yours.' He eased himself into a sitting position and grabbed hold of the rifle. 'Now,' he continued, 'perhaps you can tell me just what all this is about?'

'You is dead!' gasped the first youth. 'I saw Jed shoot you an' I saw you fall off your horse.'

'Then you'd better believe in ghosts,' grinned Caleb. 'I'd say I was very much alive. Now, I want an explanation 'cos believe me I am quite capable of blastin' you both into the next world if you don't.'

Jed gulped and pulled at his dirty neckerchief. 'You murdered our ma, pa an' two sisters,' he said hoarsely. 'We both saw you an' your cronies; we was up in the woods behind the house.'

'Now I'd say that if there had been anyone else with me you'd both've been dead by now,' said Caleb. 'As it is, you still came pretty damned close to it an' still might.' He stood up, keeping the gun pointing at the older youth. 'Now, I suggest we all go back to wherever you live, or at least move away from these trees, and then you can tell me exactly what happened. Just get one thing fixed in your minds though, whoever it was you saw, I sure wasn't one of them. Now move!'

The two youths looked at him amazed, but they said nothing as they turned and headed down a small slope, round a clump of trees and on towards the still burning remains of what had apparently been their home, a small, single-roomed, timber hovel. Two dogs lay lifeless in the yard, each still tethered to a post, and the bodies of two young women lay spreadeagled across some bales of hay, the position of their clothing leaving no room for doubt as to what had happened to them. Caleb went through the motions of ensuring that they were in fact dead—which they were, each having been dispatched by a single bullet through the front of their heads—pulled their clothes over them and then looked about for the other two bodies. He located them, one still burning, in the dying flames that had been the house.

'How long ago?' he asked the youths, who by that time had realized that this particular black man was not one of those they had seen earlier.

'About half an hour,' said the older one, Jed 'Me an' Aaron was out collectin' firewood when we heard shootin'. We ran back to the house, but we was too late, there was nothin' we could do 'cept watch, neither of us had a gun then. Ma an' Pa must've been inside the house, but we never saw them till we found their bodies, both still burnin'. There was four of 'em, all blacks, just like you, an' about the same size. They took turns with our sisters an' then shot 'em. They didn't know we was watchin'.'

'I guessed it must've been somethin' like that,' grunted Caleb. 'I reckon there's nothin' I can say other than I sure am sorry. Did you get a good look at these men, would you recognize any of them?'

Aaron shuffled uneasily. 'Look, mister, we just thought ... What I mean is, from where we saw you, you looked just like the leader, he had a hat on just like yours an' his horse could've been your horse's twin. Besides, the last time we saw a black in this part of the world was more'n two years ago an' now, suddenly, we gets five in one day. You can't blame us for bein' suspicious.'

'And the fact that I am black was enough,' smiled Caleb. 'Had they been whites and another white man had come along, you probably wouldn't've thought anything of it. So, you did get a good look at them.' He reached into his saddle-bag and pulled out a sheaf of papers and, after flicking through them, produced four which he showed to the boys. 'Recognize any of these?' he asked.

'That one for definite,' replied Jed. 'Probably that one as well.' He indicated another picture. 'I ain't too sure about the other two, but they could easily be them. The trouble is most blacks look pretty much the same to us.'

'I have the same problem with a lot of white folk,' grinned Caleb, as he glanced at the pictures, although he knew all the details by heart. 'Frank Sullivan, his brother Jacob and their cousins Winston and Grant Marshall. As mean a bunch as you could ever wish to meet who make their living by robbing out-of-the-way farmers and who always murder their victims. I heard they were in the area, but I didn't expect to see evidence of them so soon.' He also knew the value of the rewards out on the four men; $2,000 for Frank Sullivan, $1,500 for his brother, Jacob, and $1,000 on each of the other two, a total of $5,500, no mean sum and of great interest to a bounty hunter like Caleb.

'Are you some sort of lawman?' asked Aaron.

'Not exactly,' smiled Caleb. 'The only law I preach is God's law. Don't you recognize a preacher when you see one?'

'No, sir,' admitted Jed 'Nearest church is in Bullhead an' that's two days' ride. There was a preacher through this way last year sometime, but he was a monk or somethin'. Anyhow, he wore what looked like a brown dress just like a woman. If'n it hadn't been for the fact he had a beard we would've sworn he was a woman. Anyhow, he didn't seem too interested in us but Pa did catch him round the back of the barn with our sister Kate. Pa reckoned this preacher had his hand up Kate's skirts. I know the preacher lifted up his skirts an' ran like hell when Pa took down his shotgun.'

'He sounds like a Catholic priest,' grinned Caleb. 'Most of them are OK, but there are a few like the one you describe. Anyway, my name is Caleb Black, yes, Black; Black by name and black by colour. I'm a regular preacher all right, it's just that I haven't settled anywhere.'

'How come you have them Wanted posters?' asked Aaron. 'Only man I ever seen with them before is Sheriff McCready.'

'Even a preacher needs to make a living and I just happen to make mine being a bounty hunter,' said Caleb. 'Where does this Sheriff McCready live?'

'A for real bounty hunter?' asked Jed plainly very impressed. 'We ain't never had us a real bounty hunter out in these parts before. The sheriff lives out at Bullhead. This is part of his territory, but we don't see him that often, no more'n twice a year.'

'What about neighbours?' asked Caleb.

'Nearest is the Wilsons,' replied Aaron. 'They live over in the next valley, maybe an hour's ride. Then there's the Chamberlains over in the other direction, about two hours away. You must've passed their place, goin' by the direction you came from.'

'I did pass a farm,' admitted Caleb. 'Which way did these men go? It wasn't the way I came, that's for sure, I would have seen them.'

'Off down the valley,' said Aaron, pointing down the gentle slope which led away from their house. 'There's a river at the bottom an' you follow it to the left for the Wilsons an' to the right brings you back up Yermo Creek to the Chamberlain place so they could've gone back that way without you seein' 'em.'

'Maybe they could,' conceded Caleb, 'You ought to know. Which way is it to Bullhead?'

'Just follow the road up past the Wilson farm an' keep goin' for two days,' said Jed He looked at the bodies of his sisters and then smiled weakly at Caleb. 'If'n you is a preacher, maybe it'd be fittin' if'n you could say a few words for them. Ma was a religious woman; she read to us from the Bible every single day.'

'Under the circumstances, I suppose it's the least I can do,' agreed Caleb. 'You two set to digging four graves. Make them as deep as you can, wolves and foxes have a nasty habit of digging them up if they are too near the surface and it isn't a pretty sight when they've had a go at them and then the buzzards come in for their share.'

'Sure, we've seen the wolves an' buzzards

at dead deer an' things,' said Aaron. 'OK, best place is over behind the barn, the ground's easier to dig there.'

Whether it was because they had been brought up in such a remote area or because they were both naturally hardened to life, Caleb was uncertain, but he could not help but sense a certain coldness in the two young men and knew that he could never completely trust them. He made quite certain that he knew exactly where they were at any given time and that he also knew where their rifle was. This appeared to be the only weapon they had and he had noticed Jed the older boy, looking enviously at the two Colts around his waist and felt that they could quite easily kill him simply to get their hands on his guns.

Whilst the boys were digging the graves, Caleb wandered slowly around the farm, noting that the main crop appeared to be tobacco which to him looked just about ready to be harvested. The land immediately surrounding the house was given over to growing vegetables, obviously for use in the house, and in a small field was a solitary cow, three pigs—one of which looked just about ready to farrow—two goats and two draught horses. There were about two dozen hens scratching about the yard and among the vegetables. All the other cultivated land, which he estimated to be about forty acres, appeared to be given over to tobacco. Other than that the hills were a mixture of open grassland and forest.

'It looks like you've got a crop just about ready to harvest,' said Caleb, when he went to see how the graves were coming on. 'How will you manage?'

'We'll manage!' grated Jed. 'Us Joneses don't need help off no man.' Caleb smiled, if nothing else he had established that their name was Jones.

'Do you intend living here now?' Caleb asked again. 'There seems a lot of work for just the two of you.'

'An' just where the hell else are we goin' to live?' laughed Aaron, sardonically. 'Me an' Jed did most of the work anyhow. Sometimes the girls would help out in the fields, but not often. Their job was milkin' the cow an' goat an' lookin' after the pigs an' chickens. Sure, I guess we'll carry on; there sure ain't nothin' else we can do an' I guess we owns this land now. It won't take us long to cut a few timbers an' build us a new house. Until then we can live in the barn.'

'You'd be better off finding yourselves a couple of wives,' said Caleb. 'How old are you?'

'I'm eighteen,' replied Jed 'an' Aaron here is sixteen. I'd say we was both a mite young to be thinkin' about gettin' wed. Anyhow, there ain't no girls our age hereabouts. Nancy Chamberlain is the oldest an' she's only thirteen.'

'What about in Bullhead?'

'You must be jokin'!' laughed Jed. 'Them girls in Bullhead wouldn't look twice at some hick boy from the hills. Don't you go worryin' yourself none about us, Mr Preacherman, if'n we can deal with a bear I reckon we can deal with this farm.' Caleb decided to leave the matter alone and waited until the graves were deep enough.

The boys produced some old, thick, tarred cloth from the barn which they cut into pieces just large enough to wrap around each of the bodies and once again Caleb could not help but notice the apparent lack of feeling and coldness in both boys as they roughly handled the bodies of their sisters and complained that the bodies of their parents were almost too hot to handle properly. However, eventually they had all the bodies stitched up in the cloths. That coldness extended to the seemingly casual way they dumped each body in a grave and the only moment either of them appeared to show any slight sign of emotion was as Caleb, Bible in hand, said a prayer over the graves. Even that slight sign disappeared as soon as he had finished and they both set to shovelling earth back into the holes. They even laughed and joked as they were working, making comments about burying the killers of their family alive. Caleb was a man of the world and had witnessed many weird things, but even he felt a shiver run up his spine as he watched these two boys apparently treating the whole matter as one of those things that happen every day.

By the time the bodies were buried, it was almost sunset and under normal circumstances Caleb would not have considered moving on, but he really did not relish the idea of spending the night in the company of either of the Jones boys and he was quite certain that he would not have been able to sleep for fear of having his throat cut in the middle of the night. The fact that neither of them suggested that he should stay told him that they too were not very keen on the idea. He took his leave of them at the first opportunity and set off in the direction of the Wilson farm, hoping that he might receive a more welcoming reception there.

It took less than an hour to reach the Wilson farm, again growing mainly tobacco, but the reception was almost as bad as the one he had had at the Joneses. A single shot from a rifle echoed round the small hollow he was in, although this time it was plainly not intended to kill him, just to warn.

'That's about far enough!' came the command. 'State your business or turn right round an' get out of here.'

'I really do appreciate a warm welcome,' called Caleb, raising his hands to show that he was unarmed. 'I just had me a really hot welcome out at the Joneses, someone just killed everyone there except the two boys and then they burned the place down.'

A large, long-haired, bearded man stepped from behind a tree, his rifle held at his waist but aimed steadily at

Caleb. 'I heard what you said, mister,' he growled. 'Why should anyone want to kill Martha an' Ernie?'

'I admit to knowing a great many things,' smiled Caleb, 'but even my extensive knowledge does not include reading other people's minds. How should I know why? All I know is they did. The two boys, Jed and Aaron, only escaped because they were out gathering wood.'

'You must think you're somethin' of a smart ass,' snarled the man. 'Well, don't go thinkin' that all us hill folk are dumb, other folk have thought that an' soon found out otherwise.'

'The thought never entered my head,' smiled Caleb. 'My name is Caleb Black, I am a man of the cloth, a Minister of Religion. I am simply passing through the area and was wondering if you and your good wife could provide me with some food and accommodation for the night. I am quite prepared to pay if necessary. I understand that the nearest town, Bullhead, is about two days away.'

'A preacher!' muttered the man. 'Sure, you look like a preacher, leastways you dress just like the preacher in Bullhead.' He lowered his rifle slightly but Caleb took care to keep his hands raised. 'Is there some sort of meetin' of blacks goin' on?' continued the man. 'There was four others through here this afternoon. They didn't stop though, me an' the boys made sure of that.' Caleb could well believe that he and his *boys* were quite capable of making sure of almost anything.

'Are you sure you're a preacher?' asked a female voice from behind another tree. A woman, almost as large as the man, stepped out, she too holding a rifle and giving the impression that she knew how to use it and was not afraid to if necessary. 'I ain't never seen a black preacher before.'

'I've got papers to prove it,' nodded Caleb. 'I can show them to you if you like.' He still did not lower his hands, knowing full well that types like these

23

were only too ready to shoot rather than ask questions and would probably feed his body to their pigs; he had known of such things before.

'Ain't no use showin' us no papers,' grunted the man, 'none of us ain't never had no schoolin'. OK, feller, you can come on in, I don't ever want it said that a Wilson turned away a hungry man no matter what colour he was.'

Caleb breathed a sigh of relief and lowered his hands, took the reins of his horse and gently urged her forward. The man walked ahead and the woman walked behind him the 100 yards or so to the house which appeared rather larger than the Jones house. He discovered that it had three rooms, a living-room and two bedrooms. Three young men came out of the door as they approached, the eldest appearing to be about the same age as Jed Jones, the second about the same age as Aaron and the third a couple of years younger. Caleb dismounted, expecting one

24

of the boys to take his horse and lead it to the barn, but they simply stood and sullenly stared at him. He hitched the animal to a post and turned to the woman, raising his hat slightly.

'I thank you for your hospitality, ma'am,' he smiled. 'Shall I take my horse to the barn or will one of the boys do it?' The woman nodded at the youngest boy who grudgingly untied the animal and led it away. Caleb wondered if he was doing the right thing in allowing his rifle and saddle-bags out of his sight.

'What's all this about the Joneses bein' burned out?' asked Mrs Wilson.

'Burned out and murdered,' said Caleb, 'along with their two daughters. The boys, Jed and Aaron I think they're called, managed to escape. They claim it was those four black men you saw earlier and, knowing just who they are, I can well believe it.'

'Pity about Martha an' Ernie, they was good folk,' said Mr Wilson. 'If anyone should've died it should've been them boys.'

'A harsh thing to say about anyone,' said Caleb.

'Pure evil they are,' said Mrs Wilson. 'I'd've been ready to believe they killed their own folk. Are you sure it was those four blacks?'

'I am quite convinced of it,' said Caleb. 'Jed tried to kill me thinking I was one of the gang.' In actual fact he was inclined to agree with the sentiments expressed by Mrs Wilson; Jed and Aaron Jones were evil. 'I think someone ought to report what happened to the sheriff in Bullhead.'

'We're both mighty sorry for Martha, Ernie an' the girls,' said Mr Wilson, 'but it ain't no concern of ours. If anyone has to do any reportin' it has to be one of them boys, but I don't suppose either of them really give a damn about what happened.'

'They was real trouble,' added Mrs Wilson. 'Many's the leatherin' Ernie had to dole out to 'em an' they deserved every beatin' they got. Nobody could ever prove nothin', but it was known that Jed was not above messin' with his sisters.'

'Unfortunately such things do happen,' nodded Caleb. 'However, all that does not alter the fact that there are four killers on the loose in the area and it is quite possible that they will strike again; someone has to inform the sheriff.'

'If that's the way you is headin',' said Mr Wilson, 'you do it. I got me too many things to do here an' if these men are about, I sure don't fancy leavin' Mary here on her own.' Caleb had to agree that he did have a point; it would be most unwise to leave the family undefended.

'I most certainly will report the facts,' nodded Caleb. 'Now, I really would appreciate a wash. Do you have any hot water?'

'It ain't Sunday,' said Mary Wilson, apparently rather astonished that anyone should even consider washing on any day other than Sunday.

'I like to wash every day,' smiled Caleb.

'It ain't natural,' muttered Mr Wilson. 'Still, if'n that's what you want, I guess I ain't the one to stop you. There's allus a pot of hot water on the fire, you just help yourself. There's a bowl hangin' up behind the door.'

Caleb nodded his thanks and went into the house, found a large basin hanging behind the door and poured some steaming water into it and carried it outside to a pump where he cooled it. Mary Wilson even found him a piece of very hard soap, but it appeared that the only towelling they had was an old sack.

Caleb stripped to his waist and tried to ignore the family as they gathered round to watch what was apparently a strange ritual. In fact they were all rather more interested in seeing what a black man looked like stripped to the waist. When he had finished and had attempted, not very successfully, to dry himself on the sacking, Caleb smiled at them and puffed out his muscular chest. Mary Wilson seemed impressed if none of the others did.

He was told that he could either share a bed with the boys or sleep in the barn and as far as he was concerned there was no contest—the barn won and he felt that it was probably the safest place. He did not have the same feelings of mistrust of the Wilsons as he had the Jones boys, but at the same time there were still a few doubts.

An extra place was laid at the rough, wooden table and what appeared to be either pork or chicken stew placed in front of him. Quite deliberately, Caleb made a point of saying grace before he sat down. The boys had already clattered to their places on one of the wooden benches and, when Caleb made it obvious that he was about to say grace, they glanced nervously at their parents and slowly shuffled to their feet as Caleb spoke. Still uncertain as to what to do next, they all waited for the preacher to take his seat before taking theirs. From that point onwards it seemed that it was every man for himself as they grabbed at the greyish, dry bread and ripped it apart. Mary Wilson managed to salvage a reasonable sized piece for her guest. The stew turned out to be a mixture of chicken and pork and tasted very good. Some very strong coffee followed which Caleb drank more out of courtesy than the need for a drink. Later, he took some water from the pump to quench his thirst.

The sudden barking of one of the Wilsons' two dogs had everyone, including the youngest boy and Caleb, grabbing their guns and rushing to the windows and doors ...

'Hi there in the house!' came a voice from the darkness. 'It's us, Jed an' Aaron Jones Is there anyone at home?'

The scraping of steel-rimmed wheels on stones followed this greeting and eventually the dim shape of a horse drawing a buckboard could be made out. As it drew closer, two shadowy figures jumped down and came towards the house. Jim Wilson opened the door and stepped out, rifle still at the ready, and waited for the two to come nearer.

'Evenin' Mr Wilson,' greeted Jed Jones 'Glad to see that you is still all right. We had us some visitors earlier on.' Caleb shivered slightly at the casual and even jocular manner of the boy. 'Maybe you heard about it, there was a black preacherman headin' your way who knows all about it.'

'We heard,' grunted Jim Wilson. 'Sorry to hear about what happened. What can we do for you?'

'Nothin' much,' said Aaron Jones 'We got round to figurin' that maybe this black preacher either didn't come this way or passed you by an' we figured that you ought to know what happened at our place.'

'Very neighbourly,' Jim Wilson grunted

again. 'I guess you'd better come inside. Your preacher is here as well.' He stood aside to allow the two boys through the door and then followed them. Caleb noted that no member of the family had lowered their guns and then realized that neither had he. Quietly he returned his Colt to its holster.

'Hi there, Mr Black,' smiled Aaron. 'We kinda figured you'd be here.' He sniffed the air and looked in the direction of the large cooking pot hanging over the fire. 'That sure smells good, Mrs Wilson. Me an' Jed don't seem to have had the time to get round to eatin' today, it has been kinda busy.' The thought crossed Caleb's mind that the real reason for the visit was to cadge some food and not out of any concern for the Wilsons.

'I reckon the least we can do is give them some food?' said Mary Wilson to her husband, more in the form of a question than a statement. Jim Wilson nodded and the two boys clattered to

the table while Mary Wilson served up some stew in the rough, wooden bowls which had been used earlier. Any thought of washing them before re-using them did not seem to enter her head and it certainly did not appear to bother either of the Jones boys. Everyone lapsed into silence as they ate, a scene which reminded Caleb of an occasion he had spent working in a lunatic asylum where the inmates behaved more like animals than human beings, especially at meal times.

Jed Jones belched loudly and pushed his bowl to one side and wiped his mouth with the sleeve of his tattered jacket, belched again and smiled broadly. 'That was good. Thanks, Mrs Wilson. I guess one of us has got to learn how to cook from now on.'

'I'll leave that to you,' belched Aaron. 'Ma allus said I was the only one she ever knew who could burn water.'

'You is keepin' the place on then?' asked the eldest of the Wilson boys. 'Man, if'n I

was in your position I'd be off to one of the big cities.'

'You've been told you can go as soon as you is twenty-one,' scolded his mother. 'You won't though, you all know when you is well off.'

'We've been talkin' about that,' said Jed 'At first we decided that we would stay an' then we decided we wouldn't an' then we decided we would. We don't rightly know what to do. The one thing we have decided is go on into Bullhead an' see the bank or a lawyer. Pa had some papers hidden in a tin under the floorboards an' we found them after the preacher had left. They warn't burned at all. Trouble is, neither me nor Aaron ain't much good at readin'. We looked at some of the papers an' couldn't even understand the first word let alone some of them really big words. There's some numbers, too, but I can't figure out what they mean. Ma allus did things like that; Pa couldn't read either.'

'Would you like me to look at them for you?' asked Caleb. Everyone in the room looked at him in amazement.

'You can read?' queried Jim Wilson.

'You find such a thing surprising?' said Caleb. 'I was also an officer in the army during the war and I had to be able to read and write. Besides, you'd expect a Minister of Religion to be able to read, wouldn't you?'

'Not necessarily,' said Mary Wilson. 'The minister before the one they got now in Bullhead couldn't read an' write, but he knew all the gospels off by heart.'

'Most unusual,' smiled Caleb. 'They usually insist that Ministers of Religion are able to read and write.'

'Even when they is blind?' laughed Mrs Wilson. 'Sure, I reckon he could read before he went blind, but after that he had to rely on his memory.' Everyone except Caleb appeared to find this very funny.

'Do you want me to look at these

papers?' Caleb asked again, ignoring the joke.

'What ...? No, no thanks,' said Jed. 'They is private papers an' we don't want no passin' er ... er ... stranger knowin' our business.'

'And certainly not a passing black man,' smiled Caleb. 'OK, it doesn't bother me. When are you going into Bullhead?'

'In the mornin',' said Aaron, wincing as his brother's elbow jabbed into his ribs. 'Well, that was my idea, we ain't really decided,' he added. Caleb had not missed the elbow in the ribs and smiled to himself.

'That's partly why we've come over to see you, Mr Wilson,' said Jed 'It looks like we'll have to be in Bullhead for about a week all told, includin' gettin' there an' back, an' we wondered if you'd mind keepin' an eye on things at our place for a while. Mind you,' he laughed, 'there ain't that much left to keep an eye on 'ceptin' the cow an' the goat is gonna need milkin'.

I guess you can keep whatever milk you get from 'em.'

'We ain't had us decent cow's milk for almost a year,' said Mary Wilson, 'not since our old cow died.'

'I reckon it's the least we can do,' nodded Jim Wilson. 'OK, son, you is on.'

'Thanks Mr Wilson, Mrs Wilson,' said Jed. He looked at Caleb. 'If you is headed for Bullhead, maybe we'll meet up there; you might make it in less'n two days.' Caleb sincerely hoped that he would get there in under two days and that he would not encounter either of the Jones boys again, although he had the sinking feeling that he would. The other thing on his mind was the sum of $5,500, the reward for apprehending Frank Sullivan and his gang. That kind of money was just too tempting to allow to pass by.

Much to Caleb's relief and, apparently, judging by the looks on their faces, the Wilsons, Jed and Aaron took their leave and headed back to their farm. About two hours later Caleb settled in some straw in the barn, mulling over just where to start looking for the outlaws.

TWO

Mary Wilson did offer Caleb breakfast before he left, but, quite apart from the fact that he had long since abandoned the habit of eating first thing in the morning, the grey mass he was offered which masqueraded under the name of porridge was, in his opinion, enough to put anyone off eating forever. He went on his way about half an hour after sunrise.

Any consideration Caleb had given to the question of the $5,500 reward for the outlaws had been strictly limited, the very amount had dictated what his course of action would be and, as soon as he was clear of the farm, he began the task of looking for signs. However, even Caleb was among the first to admit that his tracking skills were not one of his better attributes and what he took to be clear signs on several occasions became either lost or merged with other tracks. In the end he gave up and worked on the theory that they would almost certainly be heading in the same direction he was since the natural lie of the land and hills offered very little opportunity for alternative routes.

He had been assured that it was a two-day ride to Bullhead, but he eventually realized that while it might have been two days on a mule-drawn buckboard, it certainly would not take that long riding a horse at a steady pace. Even so, he was more than surprised when, just before nightfall, he came across a sign which proclaimed that Bullhead was only another fifteen miles.

During the day he had passed several farms and had been stared at by both farmers and children, but he had not stopped nor asked them directions or how far Bullhead was and he doubted if he would have received a sensible answer since farmers rarely thought in terms of miles but in terms of time, time as measured by the pace of a mule, not a horse. He had been tempted to ask if the outlaws had passed that way, but on the one occasion he had been on the verge of doing so, the farmer had held his shotgun in such a way that made him think that perhaps it was not a good idea. He had also made rather cursory examination of the trail in the vain hope of being able to identify definite tracks, but had not succeeded.

Bullhead was reached about an hour after sunset and, from what he could see, appeared to be an average-sized town consisting of one main street and two or three side streets. Most of the stores and shops were closed; in fact the only buildings which appeared to be open were the saloon, a small hotel and the livery stable. Deciding that he would like a comfortable bed for a change, his first call was to the small hotel where the owner, a large woman of indeterminate years, looked suspiciously at him, but did eventually agree to letting one small back room.

'We don't get Negroes round these parts for years an' suddenly we gets five of you,' said the woman,

Mrs Bracewell. 'Is there some kind of convention goin' on?'

'Pure coincidence,' smiled Caleb, quite relieved to hear that the outlaws were in town. 'I can assure you that I have no connection with the others.'

'You some kind of preacher?' she asked, looking him up and down. 'You dress just like our minister does.'

'Yes,' laughed Caleb, 'I am some kind of preacher.'

'Then what you wearin' a gun for?' she demanded. 'Preachers don't wear guns.'

'This one does,' said Caleb, assuming that his answer was good enough for her. 'These other Negroes, where are they now?'

'Saloon, probably,' she muttered. 'They

never asked for rooms here an' I ain't sure I would've taken 'em in if they had. That'll be one dollar a night for the room, in advance ...' She held out a grubby hand for her money. 'How long are you stayin'?'

'I should think two nights will be long enough,' he smiled, taking some coins from his pocket and counting out the required two dollars.

'There ain't nothin' in Bullhead to make any man want to stop longer, that's for sure,' grunted Mrs Bracewell. 'I don't do no meals. If'n you want somethin' to eat the saloon can rustle up somethin' or there's an eatin'-house further down the street; but that ain't open at the moment on account of Liz Craig an' her family have been taken with some kind of fever.' Caleb smiled and wondered if the fever had been induced by the usual unsavoury cooking he had experienced in other eating-houses. 'I don't lock the place so you is free to come an' go at whatever time suits you. The saloon closes when the last customer has been thrown out on to the street, an' that's usually Sam Trickett at about midnight.'

'Is your sheriff around?' he asked. 'I heard you had one and his name is McCready.'

'Sure thing,' she nodded. 'His office is down the street next to Liz Craig's place.' She cocked her head to one side and looked at him strangely for a moment. 'What you want to know for, you tryin' to find him or avoid him?'

'I am a minister, not an outlaw,' he laughed. 'I like to make myself known to the sheriff wherever I stay as it prevents any misunderstanding. Strange as it may seem, most people tend to look upon black folk as troublemakers.'

'I'll show you to your room,' she said, rather uneasily. 'It's clean an' tidy an' I would appreciate it if you kept it that way. There's plenty of blankets an' the privy is out the back, through that door.' She indicated a door at the rear of the small hallway. 'You can have hot water for washin' if you want, that's twenty cents a jug, or you can use cold water. There's a basin an' jug in your room, that don't cost nothin' extra.'

'Just tell me when I've used that up,' smiled Caleb as he produced a dollar piece and handed it to her. 'I hate washing and shaving in cold water. I could even use a bath if you have one.'

'Bath!' exclaimed Mrs Bracewell, almost disbelieving what she had heard. 'Don't do no baths here. Jake Green, the barber, he does baths for them what wants 'em, which ain't too often from what I hear.'

'I passed his shop,' said Caleb. 'He doesn't appear to be open at the moment.'

'Closes sharp at six,' she said. 'Most places close at six an' on Sunday they don't open at all, 'ceptin' the saloon, that's allus open. Some folk did try to get that to close on Sunday as well, but they didn't succeed.' She led the way up the bare-boarded stairs and along a narrow passage at the end of which she threw open a door with a flourish. 'It's small but it should do you,' she announced. 'If it don't ... tough luck, all my other rooms is taken.' Caleb had serious doubts as to whether the hotel was fully occupied or not, but did not argue, sensing that had the hotel been even half full, Mrs Bracewell would have refused him a room. It was purely the fact that she had no other customers which had persuaded her to let him stay.

As she had said, it was a small room, just large enough to take one single bed and a chest of drawers on top of which stood a basin and jug of water. He decided that it would do for him and nodded. It certainly looked clean enough, but after she had left him, he shook out the blankets in an attempt to dislodge any livestock which might have taken up residence. Nothing obvious dropped from the blankets.

His next call was to the livery stable where, for one dollar a day, his horse was taken in and given hay, feed and water. He removed the saddle and hung it over the side of the stall, removed the saddle-bags and his rifle and then made his way down the street to the sheriff's office, where he was confronted by a rather young and somewhat nervous-looking young man.

'Sheriff McCready?' asked Caleb as he entered the office, knowing full well that the nervous smile in front of him was not Sheriff McCready.

'He's away on business,' said the young man, trying his best to appear in control and at the same time making sure that the badge which designated him as a deputy sheriff was in full view. 'Deputy Bywater at your service. What can I do for you ... er ... sir?'

'Deputy Bywater,' grinned Caleb, doffing his hat in acknowledgement. 'I had hoped to talk to Sheriff McCready. Perhaps you can tell me when he will return.'

'Could be tomorrow or it could be Friday,' replied Deputy Bywater. 'He's makin' one of his regular rounds of the county. He's got a big area to cover; he ain't just a town sheriff. There's no real way of knowin' where he is at the moment or when he will be back.' He stood up and puffed out his chest a little, accentuating his badge of office. 'I'm in charge whenever he's away. Any business you have will have to be done through me.'

Caleb smiled, shook his head and pulled up a chair opposite the desk, straddled it and rested his chin on the backrest, He made no attempt to hide the fact that he wore two guns. He dropped his saddle-bags and rifle on to the floor and then drew some posters from one of the saddle-bags and placed them on the table in front of the deputy.

'Recognize them?' he asked. Deputy Bywater looked at them for a moment and nodded. 'I thought you might,' continued Caleb. 'Have you done anything about them?'

'Such as?' asked the deputy.

'Such as arrested them?' suggested

Caleb, hoping that he had not.

'Mister,' grinned the deputy, rather weakly. 'I've been doin' this job for about nine months now and I sorta like it. I'd like to take over when Mr McCready retires so I don't go lookin' for trouble. Sure, they rode into town about midday an' I checked 'em out. We always check out any strangers who come into town. You know what they're like just as well as I do. I thought I'd leave that kind of decision up to Mr McCready when he comes back.'

'And you'll be checking me out as soon as I leave here. I thought deputies were supposed to uphold the law just like regular sheriffs,' chided Caleb. 'Especially when they are left in sole charge.'

'There's four of them, Mr ... er ...'

'Black,' smiled Caleb. 'The Reverend Caleb Black. Black by name and black by colour.'

'Reverend!' exclaimed the deputy, looking hard at Caleb's two guns.

'Reverend,' confirmed Caleb. 'I have papers to prove it if you would like to see them.'

'No, no,' said the deputy. 'I believe you, it's just that ...'

'It's just that you haven't seen a priest wearing a gun before,' interrupted Caleb. 'And you certainly haven't seen one wearing two guns before. I am an ordained Minister of Religion but I do not have a parish. I've never really wanted one since I feel I am often of more use to people in some of the more remote parts where they never see a priest. Being a wanderer means that I have to make living somehow and I discovered some time ago that one of the easier ways to earn my living was to become a bounty hunter.'

'Bounty hunter!' exclaimed the deputy, obviously surprised. 'Well, at least that explains the guns and your interest in those men.' He glanced at the Wanted posters and nodded. 'An' that amount of money would make most folk think twice.'

'Of course, if you were to arrest them it would mean that I would not be able to collect,' smiled Caleb. 'I sincerely hope that you would not consider such a thing, especially since it would mean depriving me of my livelihood.'

'I already considered it, Mr Black,' said the young man. 'But, like I said, there's four of 'em an' them kind of odds are a little too much for me. I ain't what you could call a gunfighter, although I can use a gun if I have to. Mr McCready allus says if it means you could end up dead, leave it alone no matter who or what they are. I reckon that's good advice for any man, includin' bounty hunters.'

'It's perhaps as well we all don't think like that,' smiled Caleb. 'If we did, no outlaw would ever be brought to justice. Now, I know they're not staying at Mrs Bracewell's hotel so where are they likely to be sleeping?'

'There's a bunk house out behind the livery,' said the deputy. 'Pretty rough place, but it seems to suit most travellers an' most of the farmers who head this way. The charge is twenty-five cents a night without food, fifty cents with, but I sure wouldn't recommend either.'

'And the chances are that at this moment they are in the saloon,' said Caleb. He stood up and picked up his bags and rifle. 'You obviously haven't heard yet, but I think you will be hearing soon. It appears that these men have murdered a family named Jones; I don't know just where they live apart from the fact that it is a good day back along the trail. The two sons of the family survived and I believe they are on their way to Bullhead at this moment.'

'The Joneses!' responded the deputy. 'I wouldn't've thought anyone could've caught old Ernie by surprise. How do you know all this?'

'I was through there yesterday and the boys—I think they're called Aaron and Jed—tried to kill me. I gave them the benefit of the doubt when they claimed they mistook me for one of the outlaws.'

Deputy Mick Bywater was plainly out of his depth and thought for a moment. 'Well, there ain't nothin' I can do about it on your say-so alone. Maybe when Jed an' Aaron tell me, I can. I guess it'll be official then.'

'I might just take a look in the saloon after I've dropped these back at the hotel.' A look of alarm spread across Deputy Bywater's face and Caleb grinned. 'Don't worry, I shan't do anything which will upset the routine of this town—not tonight at least. For the moment I am simply doing what you do, checking out the opposition. Thank you for your help, Deputy, but if you really do want peace and quiet, I wouldn't mention this conversation to anyone, except Sheriff McCready should he return. By the way, I hope you noticed that the reward is for the delivery of the bodies dead or alive. As a matter of course, wherever possible, I prefer to deliver in the former state ...' Deputy Bywater looked puzzled. 'Dead!' added Caleb with a grin. 'It saves a lot of bother in the end.'

'Are you sure you is a preacher?' grunted the deputy. 'OK, Mr Preacher Bounty Hunter, I don't mind an' I'm sure Mr McCready would agree with you, he always did say the only good outlaw was a dead one. Don't worry, I won't say a word to nobody.'

Caleb nodded and left the office.

Having deposited his saddle-bags, rifle and his two Colts in his room, hidden under a loose floorboard, Caleb slowly made his way to the saloon. It was most unusual for him to go anywhere unarmed, but he had noticed that none of the citizens he had seen, apart from Deputy Bywater, wore guns and for him to wear his would make him stand out as potential trouble, especially to the four outlaws.

The fact that the citizens of Bullhead did not wear guns was nothing unusual.

It was very rare for any townsfolk, farmers or even cowhands to carry handguns, even if they could afford one, which few could. In such places shotguns or the occasional rifle were the norm and of far more use.

The arrival of yet another black man in the saloon seemed to cause something of a stir. The arrival of the first four had been a rare enough occurrence and the fact that they all wore guns immediately marked them out for what they were, although nobody dared to do anything about it. The arrival of Caleb had the effect of making a few customers decide that it was about time they went home to their wives and families a little ahead of their normal time. Most, however, felt compelled to remain where they were for no other reason than pure curiosity. The four outlaws turned and grinned at Caleb as he went to the counter and ordered a beer.

'Well now, brother,' grinned the tallest of the four, whom Caleb recognized as

Frank Sullivan. 'You is the first friendly face we seen in months. Let me pay for that beer.' He looked Caleb up and down for a moment. 'You look like a preacher.'

'Which is what I am,' nodded Caleb. 'The Reverend Caleb Black at your service.' He announced himself loud enough for everyone in the room to hear and a slight buzz went round. 'Black by name and, like you, black by colour.' Frank Sullivan threw a coin on the counter and Caleb picked up his beer and acknowledged the four of them. 'Your good health, gentlemen. It is most unusual to find other black faces in these parts. To whom do I have the pleasure of speaking?' The four of them glanced at each other for a second before Frank Sullivan replied.

'Me an' him is Frank an' Jacob Smith,' grinned Frank, nodding to the man on his right. 'We is brothers. These two are our cousins, Winston an' Grant Jones.'

'Good old-fashioned names,' smiled Caleb. 'What brings the brothers Smith and the cousins Jones to these parts?'

'Nothin' much,' said Jacob. 'We is just passin' through on our way north. What brings you this way? I wouldn't've thought this was the type of country which needed the services of a black preacher.'

'They don't and, like you, I am just passing through,' grinned Caleb. 'When do you intend moving on?'

'Maybe tomorrow, maybe the next day,' said Winston Marshall. 'What you wanna know for?' Of the four of them he appeared to be the most suspicious.

'I thought that perhaps we could travel together,' said Caleb. 'I do get rather fed up with my own company sometimes.' The four looked at each other briefly.

'Maybe we could,' nodded Frank, 'We'll think about it. Normally we don't travel with nobody else.'

'An' I got a thing against gettin' too close to preachers,' added Grant Marshall.

'An' I got me this feelin' that I ought to know who you is,' said Winston Marshall.

'Don't ask me why, but I get the feelin' that I've heard your name before. I'll remember where eventually, but I have me this feelin' that what I heard ain't all good news.'

'You have a lot of feelings,' grinned Caleb. 'It is quite possible that you have heard or even met me before. Where are you from?'

'Small place called Alligator Creek,' said Frank, 'That's down in ...'

'I know it. Then that is probably where you have heard of me,' smiled Caleb. He did in fact know Alligator Creek, having conducted two weddings, a christening and a funeral there a few years earlier. He struggled to remember the names. 'I married two couples there. I think one of the men was called Bennett, Royston Bennett and the woman Thelma—Thelma White. I buried an old man named James Willard, or something like that.'

Frank Sullivan slapped Caleb across the shoulder. 'Sure, we know Royston an'

Thelma an' Jimmy Willard was my uncle.' He laughed at Winston. 'That explains where you heard about him.'

'Naw!' scowled Winston. 'There's more to it than that. I was in prison when Thelma an' Royston was wed. I heard the name somewhere else, I know it. Give me time an' I'll think of it.'

Caleb was quite determined that Winston would not have the time to think, the last thing he wanted was any of them knowing what he really did until the moment came to collect. He changed the subject and for the next few minutes they engaged in idle chatter, but Caleb could sense that Winston was searching his memory for any clue as to where he had come across his name before. Eventually he bade them a good night and returned to his room at the hotel, where he, too, searched his memory for any possible clues as to where he might have come across Winston Marshall before, but he could not think of any occasion.

As a precaution, he took his guns out

of their hiding place, checked them and placed them strategically just in case he should need to react quickly during the night. He knew that a man like Winston Marshall would not hesitate to break into the room and kill him if he felt at all threatened.

The night did pass peacefully enough, even though Caleb appeared to spend most of it starting at the slightest sound. Just after dawn he went to see Deputy Sheriff Mick Bywater and explained to him what had happened the previous night. The deputy seemed largely uninterested in Caleb and his problems and was plainly quite intent on steering clear of any possible conflict.

The next thing Caleb did was to check with the livery owner, who also owned the bunkhouse, and discovered that the four outlaws had apparently decided to leave that day, but were at that moment eating their breakfast. Caleb, still unarmed, went along to the bunkhouse just in time to find the four struggling out with their gear and heading for the livery.

'Decided to leave early?' he asked. 'You don't want my company then?'

'Naw,' drawled Frank Sullivan. 'We talked about it but Grant ain't too happy about havin' a preacher along an' Winston just can't get you out of his mind. He ain't decided where he's heard of you before, but he sure don't trust you, that's for sure. Ain't that right, Winston?'

'Too damned right,' growled Winston. 'You is bad news, Mr Preacherman, I just know it, so I figure the quicker we're the hell out of here the better.'

'A pity,' shrugged Caleb. 'Perhaps it's as well though, I would hate to force my company on anyone who didn't want it. Perhaps we shall meet again.'

'Not if I have anythin' to do with it,' snapped Winston. 'C'mon, we ain't got time to stand around jawin'.' The others nodded at Caleb and went to retrieve their horses.

Caleb walked quickly back to the hotel where he donned his guns, gave the outlaws enough time to saddle their horses and leave town and then returned to the livery to saddle his own horse. Fifteen minutes later he, too, rode slowly out of town, having learned which way they went from the livery owner.

He did not travel too fast just in case he should come across them unexpectedly, or they suspected something and were lying in wait somewhere. That latter fear appeared groundless as, about two miles out of Bullhead and from the top of a ridge, he looked down the trail and saw them no more than half a mile ahead.

From that point onwards he made sure that he maintained a reasonable distance, not really knowing what his next move would be, but for the moment the terrain did not offer much scope of surprising them. He reasoned that his best chance would come if and when they stopped for a rest.

They did stop once before midday, alongside a small river, but they were in a large area of open ground and there was no chance of Caleb getting anywhere near them and he had to be content to sit and wait. He might have been able to use his rifle as they were certainly within range, but he knew that he would only get one shot and while he would probably kill one of them, he would stand no chance of taking the others. He had little alternative but to bide his time.

THREE

Half an hour later, the outlaws moved on and Caleb allowed them about ten minutes before he followed. The countryside had changed since they had left Bullhead; whereas before it had been wooded valleys interspersed with open grassland, now it had become far less wooded and the grass had taken on a more brownish hue. A herd of cattle in the distance indicated they had entered ranching territory.

At about mid-afternoon, Caleb was suddenly aware that the men in front of him had stopped and were apparently very interested in something that lay ahead. A slight detour to the top of a nearby ridge gave him a good view of what was the centre of their attention whilst at the same time keeping him out of sight.

The object of their interest appeared to be a small farm about 300 yards in front of them and, knowing just who they were and the way their minds worked, he had a pretty good idea of just what they were contemplating. After a short time, they began to move slowly towards the farm, each having drawn either rifle or handgun. He moved back down the slope and rejoined the trail, this time with rather more urgency than before.

When they eventually came into his sight again, they were no more than fifty yards from the farm and their approach was being greeted by the furious barking of a large dog which, fortunately for them and probably the dog, appeared to be securely tethered to the corner of the building. Apart from the dog there was no other sign of life and the outlaws approached the building unchallenged.

The first thing the outlaws did was to kick in the door of the house and then three of them cautiously made a circle of the premises, searched a small barn and then returned to the front of the house and went inside. This was the opportunity for Caleb to dismount and race round the back of the farm unseen. He positioned himself just inside the small barn where he waited and listened, deciding on what he would do next.

Any immediate decision on his part was suddenly put on hold as three people, a woman, an older man and a teenaged boy suddenly appeared from a small group of trees. They stopped when they saw the four horses and the older man barked an order at the other two and took a firm grasp of the shotgun he was carrying. Caleb was ready, knowing that a shotgun would be of little use against four well-armed outlaws. The man cautiously approached, shouted something which Caleb did not quite hear, but he was aware that someone must have come out of the house. He moved silently and quickly to a better vantage point.

'An' just what the hell do you think

you're up to?' he heard the man demand. 'This is private property.'

'Now that don't sound very neighbourly,' drawled a voice. 'We're hungry an' tired of travellin'; we figured we'd rest up here for the night.'

'We ain't got no food for the likes of you,' replied the farmer. 'You'd better get off my land before I use this gun.'

'You threatenin' us?' laughed another voice. 'Reckon you can force four of us off? You sure can try if'n you want to.'

The farmer had raised the shotgun to his shoulder, but the appearance of three other men made him falter and lower it. From where Caleb was he had clear view of them all, but they were obviously more interested in what they were doing and plainly did not expect anyone else to be around.

'I seen you with a woman,' said another voice. 'You'd better tell her to come out an' rustle up some food.'

'An' if I don't?' demanded the farmer.

The answer was a single shot which obviously hit the farmer, but not fatally although he did fall to the ground. His wife suddenly ran from the cover of the trees, screaming at the top of her voice. She was closely followed by the boy who grabbed his father's shotgun and pointed it threateningly. The four outlaws simply laughed. The farmer managed to struggle off the ground and clutched at his upper arm.

'You heard what we said, woman!' shouted Frank Sullivan. 'We want some food. We know you got some, we seen it. The trouble is none of us is much good at cookin'. Don't worry about your old man, he ain't hurt that bad; he'll live. You just come an' get us some food.'

The woman said something to her husband and then walked slowly towards the house. The man took the shotgun from the boy and they, too, slowly made their way into the house. Caleb moved a little closer, taking up a position behind a broken buckboard only a few yards from the front door.

'You leave her alone!' he heard the farmer shout. 'You want food, OK, you take all the food we got, but you lay one finger on my wife an' I'll kill you all.' This comment was obviously considered funny by the outlaws and they laughed. This was followed by a scream of protest from the woman.

'Leave it,' Caleb heard Frank Sullivan order. 'First things first, let her cook somethin'. After that she's fair game for us all.'

Caleb moved even closer, this time taking up position beneath a window. Cautiously he peered through the grimy glass and saw the woman now at the stove, the boy crouched in a corner under the watchful eye of Winston Marshall. The man was slumped in a rocking chair nursing his wound. Three of the outlaws had their backs towards Caleb, only Frank Sullivan was facing him.

Shooting the outlaws was a comparatively easy task, confined as they were. The only problem was that the family were likely to get killed either in the crossfire or as a deliberate act or, more likely, used as hostages. He dropped back out of sight, deciding that the best time to take them would be when they eventually sat down for their meal. He moved his position round the corner of the building just in case any one of them should venture outside.

From where he was, Caleb could hear them talking and, although he could not make out exactly what was said, it was quite clear that the outlaws were demanding to know if there was any money in the house. The reply seemed to be that there was not which certainly did not satisfy them. Ten minutes later, he heard the woman announce that the food was ready and he heard the scraping of chairs as they seated themselves at the table. He checked his rifle and handguns once again and decided that it was now or never.

He crept round to the window once again, briefly checked that all the men were at the table, and then made his way to the open door. The dog was still barking furiously and Jacob Sullivan ordered the boy to go out and shut the dog up but not to go out of his sight. The boy struggled to his feet, looked questioningly at his mother who was now tending her husband's wound. She nodded briefly and the boy went to the door.

'Quiet, Sam!' he shouted at the dog. 'Quiet, it's gonna be all right.' Suddenly he was hauled to one side and thrown to the ground as Caleb grabbed his arm and then filled the doorway with his own body, a risky manoeuvre but one he had no alternative but to take, relying solely on the element of surprise. Two shots rang out, one of the outlaws crashed to the floor and the woman screamed. Caleb kicked backwards as the boy tried to tackle him, a kick which plainly hurt.

'Don't nobody move!' commanded Caleb. 'First man to move ends up dead just like Jacob.'

Frank Sullivan and his men were hard men, not afraid of fighting or killing, but they were also wise enough to know when they were outgunned. The three of them raised their arms without being ordered to. A sneering grin slowly spread across the face of Frank Sullivan.

'The Reverend Black,' he laughed. 'I guess we should've listened to Winston, he said you were bad news.'

'Now I know where I heard of him,' snarled Winston. 'Caleb Black, bounty hunter. Sure I know you is also a preacher, but I heard about you while I was in prison. I met more'n one who'd been put there by you.'

'Bounty hunter!' exclaimed Frank. 'Yeh, I shoulda figured somethin' like that. OK, Mr Preacherman, or whatever you choose to call yourself, you got the advantage. What you gonna do now?'

'Lady,' Caleb said to the woman, ignoring Frank, 'the first thing you can do is tell that there son of yours to watch what he's doing. I know he's behind me holding an iron bar or something. You just tell him to be careful I am not an outlaw like these four. You heard him say I was a bounty hunter; it's them you've got to worry about, not me.'

'Jonathan!' called the woman. 'Don't you go doin' nothin' stupid now.'

'That's better,' smiled Caleb. 'Now, lady, you just go round that table and take all their guns and knives and bring them over here. Don't any of you even think about using her as protection, I'm mean enough to kill by shooting you through her body. You can all stand up and hand your guns and knives over to her. Oh, and lady, don't forget the one on the floor, he's got a handgun and two knives.' The woman nodded obediently and took the weapons as they were handed to her and then carried them over to Caleb. He

73

looked at her, tried to smile reassuringly, but felt that he had failed miserably. He moved further into the room. 'Jonathan!' he suddenly called out to the boy behind him. 'You just go and run your hands over their bodies; I wouldn't put it past any one of them to have a knife or even a gun hidden round their balls.' The boy looked at his mother who nodded, and went to search the men, but did not find any more weapons.

'OK,' grinned Frank Sullivan. 'What now?'

'What now is that I make sure none of you can escape,' said Caleb. 'I need some stout twine or thin rope,' he said to the woman.

'There's some in the barn,' said the farmer, the shock of what had happened apparently making him forget about his injury, which was little more than a deep graze. 'Jonathan, you go an' fetch it. Go on!' he added, seeing his son falter and look at his mother. 'Do what the man asks, go get the rope.' The boy gulped and ran from the house.

'Now, the three of you,' ordered Caleb. 'Up against that wall and keep your hands where I can see them.' They did as they were told and a couple of minutes later Jonathan returned with the rope and twine. 'Reckon you can tie them up, boy?' said Caleb.

'Sure thing, mister,' croaked Jonathan.

'Then start with him on the end,' said Caleb. 'Make sure you do a good job of it, we don't want them breaking loose.'

Ten minutes later, the three outlaws were standing with their hands tied behind their backs and only then did Caleb move forward, his gun still in his hand, to check that they really were well and truly tied. He was very satisfied; Jonathan had made a good job of it. He ordered the three to sit on the floor and proceeded to tie their ankles. Eventually he was satisfied, stood up and holstered his gun.

In the meantime, the woman had been

examining Jacob and confirmed that he was dead. She looked up questioningly at Caleb. 'Now will you please explain just what is going on?' she asked. 'Who are these men and, more importantly, who are you?'

'Like the man said,' grinned Caleb, 'the Reverend Caleb Black at your service, part-time preacher and more-or-less full-time bounty hunter. These men are wanted for a number of crimes, most of which include murder and rape. I don't know if you know the family or not, but the last thing they did was to murder Mr and Mrs Jones and their two daughters. They live on the other side of Bullhead. Oh, and just for good measure, they burned down the farm. The two Jones boys, Jed and Aaron, were lucky, they weren't there at the time.'

'I met Ernie Jones a couple of times,' said the man. 'Murdered, you say?'

The woman shuddered. 'It's lucky for us you were around,' she said. 'We could all have been dead by now.'

'Nothing more certain,' confirmed Caleb. 'It's too late now to even think about starting back to Bullhead, we'll have to stay here the night and leave first thing in the morning.' He turned to the boy. 'Jonathan, you go and get their horses and unsaddle them. Then you can go and find mine; she's tethered to a big oak tree up behind the farm somewhere. She shouldn't be too difficult to find.'

'Yes, sir,' said the boy. 'I know which tree you mean.' He looked at the body of Jacob Sullivan. 'What about him, you want a hand takin' him outside?'

'Well I'm sure your ma doesn't want to be walking over him all night,' Caleb grinned. 'OK, boy, we'll put him in the barn.' They picked up the body, Caleb taking the shoulders and Jonathan the feet, and carried him to the barn.

When Caleb returned, the man stood up and extended his hand which Caleb took. 'I guess we owe you,' he said.

'Cy Williams is the name. This is my wife Mary, the boy's name you already know. Is that straight up about you bein' a minister?'

'Straight up!' Caleb laughed. 'I took up bounty hunting because even a Minister of Religion who has no regular parish has to live somehow. I've been following these men ever since they burned down the Jones farm. All I have to do now is get them back to Bullhead. But that shouldn't be too difficult, I had to take six men for a week once. They soon found out I couldn't be messed about with.'

'I guess if you need help I could go along with you,' Cy suggested.

'I'll manage,' said Caleb. He looked at the three men sitting on the floor and laughed. 'You won't give me any trouble will you?' he said. 'The one thing you'd better know is that where the reward is for dead or alive, I normally only take in dead, so unless you want to end up that way, you'd better do as you're told.'

'You ain't got us back there yet,' scowled Frank Sullivan. 'The one thing you'd better know is that any man who kills one of us is marked for life.'

'I would suggest that hanging will be your eventual fate,' said Caleb. 'Now, I'm sure Mrs Williams doesn't want you cluttering up her house, so I'm going to tie you up in the barn, and believe me, I am very efficient at making sure people can't escape so you needn't try, but I suppose you will. On your feet.'

'How the hell are we supposed to get there?' demanded Winston Marshall. 'You'll have to untie our feet.'

'Pretend you are kids again, playing hopscotch or something,' Caleb laughed. 'You can hop all the way. Now move!'

The men struggled to their feet and, with Caleb holding the door open, they slowly hopped their way to the barn, each falling down several times on the way. Eventually Caleb had them where he wanted them, sitting against uprights and, after looking around for something suitable to tie them to the uprights with, produced a coil of wire.

'This should keep you quiet,' he grinned. 'I used to wire prisoners when I was in the army. It can be very painful if you move too much.'

He found a pair of wire cutters behind the door and snipped off various lengths. One length he threaded between their arms and their bodies, looping it round just above their elbows and then tying it behind the upright. Another length he wound round their necks and the upright, not too tight, but tight enough to be uncomfortable and painful if they struggled too much.

'That ought to keep you quiet,' he said, after he had double checked everything. 'Now, I'll go and see what Mrs Williams has for me.'

'What about us?' croaked Grant Marshall.

'You'll live a few days without food,'

grinned Caleb. 'If you are lucky I'll come and give you a drink of water later.'

'I want a piss!' complained Winston.

'Then you'll just have to wet yourself,' grinned Caleb.

'You'll suffer for this,' muttered Frank Sullivan. 'You'll never get us back.'

'Gentlemen,' said Caleb, 'I can assure you that you are very fortunate to be still alive. It is my normal policy only to take in dead outlaws, but circumstances unfortunately prevented me from killing you all. However, if you insist, it can easily be arranged that you are returned to Bullhead very dead.'

'I didn't think preachers were supposed to kill,' said Grant Marshall.

'I am from the school of an eye for an eye,' said Caleb.

'You'd kill us in cold blood?' queried Frank Sullivan.

'You'd better believe it,' Caleb said as he left the barn. 'Such things are not the sole preserve of men like you. I know of many

81

lawmen who will only shoot someone in the back.'

In fact, Caleb was not at all certain that his conscience would allow him to kill an unarmed and trussed man. He had never been called upon to make that decision and sincerely hoped that he never would.

Mary Williams appeared to have prepared something very special for the occasion, although Caleb did have difficulty in identifying exactly what the meat was. However, it tasted very good and it was only after he had eaten and was sitting outside on a bench with Cy Williams that he discovered just what he had eaten. Had he known before he might well have not enjoyed it too much.

'Possum!' announced Cy. 'Ain't no shortage of possums hereabouts an' they do a lot of damage. The only good possum is a dead one. They ain't bad eatin' either, leastways they is cheap.'

'To the best of my knowledge I have never eaten it before,' admitted Caleb. 'Mind you, when I was in the army we could have been eating anything. No matter what it was supposed to be, it always tasted the same—disgusting. I must admit though that that was very good.'

Cy pulled a small wooden box from his shirt pocket and produced two thin cheroots, one of which he handed to Caleb. Although not a regular smoker, Caleb accepted the offering and choked slightly as Cy lit it for him.

'They is a bit on the strong side,' Cy grunted. 'We grow the tobacco ourselves, not much, only a few plants for our own use, not like they do back where the Joneses come from. There that's the main cash crop.'

'And yours?' asked Caleb, more out of politeness than curiosity.

'Taters, turnips an' carrots,' puffed Cy. 'We sells most to Bullhead. It ain't much, but it keeps us goin' an' me an' Mary like it out here. We been here twenty years now.'

'Do you get much trouble?' Caleb asked.

'In all that time this is the first,' grunted Cy. 'We gets strangers through sometimes, but mostly they is doin' nothin' more'n passin' through an' they don't normally stop. We had us a pregnant woman through last year, gave birth to a girl right there in our bedroom. They moved on the next day.'

'Well, for an area which doesn't have much trouble,' said Caleb, 'I couldn't help but notice that folk appeared very wary, even downright unfriendly. They all made sure I saw they had guns when they saw me.'

'They is worse the far side of Bullhead for that,' nodded Cy. 'Tobacco farmers never trust nobody. Anyhow, we don't get Negroes in these parts all that much an' folk tend to mistrust anyone what don't look like them. They don't mean no harm, but they is best left alone.'

'They'll mistrust us even more after what those four did to the Joneses,' nodded Caleb.

Cy glanced at Caleb and smiled slightly. 'Have you met the Reverend Peter Manston, he's the minister in Bullhead?' Caleb shook his head. 'You an' him would make a fine pair. He's allus preachin' hell fire an' damnation, an' goin' on about evil-doers bein' the scourge of the earth an' how they all ought to be trampled into the dust.' He laughed sardonically. 'Seems to me that's all he does though, talk an' preach about it. He always leaves the actual dealing with things like that to others.'

'I know the type,' smiled Caleb. 'I had intended to make myself known to him, but things happened quicker than I had expected.'

'Just one thing,' nodded Cy. 'I'd advise you not to trust the man too far. Most folk accept him as a minister, but there's very few who are what you might call friendly with him. He ain't married, an' I hear tell that he's not above lettin' his hands wander when he's alone with either a woman or a young boy. One or the other I could understand, but not both.'

'It takes all sorts, I guess,' smiled Caleb. 'If you don't mind, I'll be turning in. Your wife offered to make up a bed for me in the house, but I'll be fine in the barn where I can keep an eye on those men. I'll take them a drink of water.'

'We're always up at dawn,' nodded Cy. 'See you then.'

FOUR

It was half an hour after sunrise before Caleb had the outlaws astride their horses, their hands now bound to the horns of their saddles and, as a precaution, a length of rope was tied to one ankle, passed under the horse and then tied to the other ankle.

'Don't you go falling off now,' he laughed. 'It could be you'll spook the horse and get dragged underneath.'

'We ain't likely to fall off with our hands tied like this,' complained Frank Sullivan. 'You can't keep us like this all day though, you'll have to let us loose sometime or another.'

'Who can't?' laughed Caleb. 'We'll make Bullhead by evening, you can manage until then.'

87

The body of Jacob Sullivan was tied
across his horse and covered in a water-
proof, mainly to keep the flies at bay,
which, even at that time of the morning,
had sensed death and were now hovering
round the body. Eventually, Caleb was
satisfied with the arrangements and, with
the four horses in a line behind him, the
lead horse tethered to his saddle, the one
carrying Jacob bringing up the rear, he
rode away from the Williams farm.

The sky was overcast but it was a good
day for riding, not too hot and not too
cold. For the first half-hour there was a
barrage of complaints from the three men
which Caleb totally ignored. Eventually,
realizing the futility of complaining, the
men lapsed into silence apart from the
occasional comment. A halt was called
for a short time at midday, when Caleb
allowed one man at a time off his horse
to attend the calls of nature and to stretch
aching limbs. He also allowed each man
to drink from a small river, but refused

all pleas to be allowed to rest for longer.

'You is a dead man,' sneered Frank Sullivan. 'Even if you do get us locked up in jail, we ain't found one yet which can hold us an' we got friends who'll make it their business to see that we don't an' who'll come after you.'

'Now I know you're lying!' laughed Caleb. 'Men like you simply do not have any friends.'

'Then I'll kill you myself,' snarled Frank.

Caleb sighed and then laughed. 'You know, you have no gratitude at all. This is something I don't normally do, take in men alive. It would be a very simple thing for me to alter things and I don't think anyone would ask too many questions.'

'You wouldn't dare!' Frank challenged.

'Don't be too sure about that!' grinned Caleb, drawing his Colt and, placing it against Frank's head, pulled back the hammer. Frank Sullivan was plainly not too sure as he glanced sideways at the gun and began to sweat. Caleb laughed again and eased the hammer down and lowered the gun.

'You got it all wrong, Reveren',' said Winston Marshall, 'us black folk should be stickin' together; we got enough problems without fightin' each other.'

'I'll say "amen" to that,' said Caleb. 'The thing is though, five thousand in black money and five thousand in white money is still five thousand; storekeepers and banks have no way of knowing which is which.'

'You'll never live to spend it!' growled Frank Sullivan.

As predicted, Bullhead was reached at just about five o'clock and this time Sheriff McCready was there to greet them. News of their impending arrival had reached the town well ahead of them, although Caleb was ready to swear that he had seen nobody along the trail and certainly nobody who could have reached Bullhead before them. However, the fact remained that the entire population of Bullhead knew of their approach long before they arrived and Caleb could not help but marvel at the efficiency of whatever telegraph system was employed.

Between Caleb leaving Bullhead the previous day and his return, Jed and Aaron Jones had arrived and had told everyone they had met what had happened at their farm. With almost every telling the whole episode took on new and very different dimensions and the brothers appeared to be relishing the attention they were now receiving. The crowd which greeted Caleb and his prisoners proved very rowdy and extremely hostile and, had it not been for the intervention of Sheriff McCready, there was little doubt that Caleb would have had the men taken from him and hanged from the nearest tree.

'It'd've saved a whole lot of bother if you'd brought 'em all in dead,' said the sheriff after he had locked the men in his cells. 'You must be the preacher,

Caleb Black. Sorry I wasn't here before. I thought my deputy must've got the story wrong, but I see now that he hadn't. I suppose you'll be wanting to collect the reward now.'

'As soon as possible,' nodded Caleb.

'Well it's goin' to take at least a week,' said the sheriff. 'I know who these men are, but before the governor's office will authorize payment, they have to be certain. They're sendin' a man out to identify them; he should be here in a few days.'

'I usually have to wait for rewards of that size,' nodded Caleb, 'but it's worth it. What happens to them now?'

'Hopefully, whoever they send will also take them back with him,' replied the sheriff. 'If they don't it means that I shall have to escort them and that's a job I can always do without. Now, maybe you'd better tell me just how you caught 'em.'

Caleb told the sheriff everything that had happened since he first encountered the Jones brothers until the moment he rode back into Bullhead, even to his concerns that the brothers appeared to show very little emotion or feeling for what had happened to their parents and sisters.

'Strange family,' nodded the sheriff. 'It was rumoured that the eldest girl had a baby a couple of months ago, but there never was any sign of one. It was also said that the father was probably her brother Jed. I wouldn't put anythin' past that family. Such things might be illegal, but there just ain't no way of doin' anythin' about it. Still, that's all in the past, poor wench is apparently dead now.'

'I supervised the burial of all the family,' confirmed Caleb. 'I must confess that I find the brothers Jones rather disturbing. I have never met anyone before who did not show some sign of grief when someone as close as their parents died, and to this pair it seemed almost like a joke—a very sick joke.'

'And they could be a problem,' nodded McCready. 'Right now they have almost the entire county on their side, bayin' for blood. I guess it was lucky I was here when you brought 'em in. If I hadn't, I think there would have been a lynchin' for sure.'

'Well, I've done my bit,' said Caleb. 'I guess I'll go and re-book my room at Mrs Bracewell's hotel, unless she's let all her rooms while I was away.'

'Empty!' declared the sheriff. 'But then she nearly always is empty; we don't get many folk passing through Bullhead. One or two of the farmers use her when they come into town, but mostly it's their wives who seem to think it grand to be able to say they're stayin' at the hotel.'

Mrs Bracewell was obviously bursting with questions as she gave Caleb the key to his room and pocketed a five-dollar advance rental plus another five dollars for the supply of hot water for the next few days, but to her credit she did not bombard him with them all at once. After he had settled in, stabled his horse and hidden his guns, Caleb made his way to the sole place of entertainment in the town, the saloon. He was somewhat surprised to discover that the entertainment for the evening included a pianist and a couple of well-worn dancing girls on the very tiny stage. The pianist was not too bad, coping quite well with the few notes which were missing and the patrons appeared to appreciate the dancing girls if Caleb did not. He had been in the bar about twenty minutes when the Jones brothers approached him.

'Nice piece of work, bringin' them outlaws in,' drawled Aaron. 'I hear they is worth about five thousand dollars.'

'Something like that,' nodded Caleb.

'Just the kind of money a man should be sharin' with the folk who earned him that kind of money,' said Jed.

'And who might that be?' smiled Caleb, knowing full well what was meant.

'Me an' Aaron, of course,' said Jed, noisily drinking his beer. 'It was our ma

95

an' pa an' sisters what was murdered by them outlaws. If they hadn't been you'd never've been any the wiser.'

There was a certain amount of logic to what Jed said and while in the past he had given most of the reward to the families of such victims' he felt no compulsion to do the same with Jed and Aaron Jones

'It was me who took all the risks,' he pointed out. 'I could just as easily have been killed.'

'Sure, but you weren't,' grinned Aaron. Both boys drained their glasses and placed them pointedly on the counter and looked expectantly at the preacher. just as pointedly Caleb turned, glass in hand, and seated himself at an empty table. The brothers said something which he did not quite catch but was well aware was not at all complimentary to either Ministers of Religion or people whose skin colour was not white.

He remained in the saloon for about another half-hour before becoming bored with the whole thing and deciding to return to his room.

Mrs Bracewell offered to make Caleb some breakfast since the saloon was not open for business before about midday and Liz Craig's eating-house was still closed, but she seemed rather relieved when Caleb refused on the grounds that he never ate breakfast. Her attitude towards him had softened, especially since discovering that he was likely to gain to the tune of $5,500 for capturing the outlaws. She even offered to return the five dollars he had paid in advance for hot water and gave hints that she was prepared to search out her old zinc bath and, if he wanted, would even scrub his back. Again Caleb refused and opted to go and see Jake Green, the barber, who had a small room at the rear of his shop where baths were available for fifty cents. He, too, had heard about the money Caleb was coming into, but even so he insisted on the fifty-cent charge. Caleb willingly paid up.

It had been about four weeks since Caleb had immersed himself in hot water and he made the most of the opportunity, even smiling at the remarks of one customer that he was fighting a losing battle if he wanted to scrub all the black off him. After his bath, he wandered down to the church where he introduced himself to the minister, the Reverend Peter Manston. He was surprised to discover that they both represented the same church. They may have had common ground on that score but it was soon obvious that they had little else in common. It was plain from the start that the Reverend Manston firmly believed that enslavement of the blacks was a perfectly proper thing and even claimed support for this belief from certain references in the Bible.

When he eventually left the church, Caleb saw that a large crowd had gathered outside the sheriff's office and it was obvious that they were after one thing: the lynching of the three outlaws. As he had expected, the brothers Jones appeared to be the ringleaders. Caleb could simply have ignored what was going on since really it was nothing to do with him, but in a sense he felt that it was he who was responsible by bringing the outlaws in. He pushed his way to front of the crowd and hammered on the door of the office, which was eventually opened by Deputy Sheriff Mick Bywater.

'Need any help?' asked Caleb. 'This lot out here don't seem too friendly.'

'It's Mr Black,' the deputy said, turning his head slightly. 'Do I let him in?'

'Why not?' came the reply. 'Right now I need all the help I can get.' The deputy stood aside and, amid boos and catcalls from the crowd, Caleb went in. 'I hope you've come to offer some assistance and not to gawp,' continued Sheriff McCready as the door closed.

'Do they mean it?' Caleb asked, looking

out of the window. 'I see a few of them have shotguns or rifles.'

'I wouldn't really know,' admitted McCready. 'I've never had anythin' like this happen before. It's the Jones boys who are whippin' 'em up, but then I guess they do have some right to feel the way they do.'

'I'm not so sure that they feel anything,' smiled Caleb. 'Right now they're the centre of attention and that's all that seems to matter to them.'

'More'n like,' admitted McCready. 'More to the point, they seem to have most of the county behind them. This is the first time anythin' like the murder of the Jones family has happened in this county for more'n twenty years an' they want instant justice.'

'Can you hold them off?' Caleb asked.

'If you are prepared to help, I don't see any real difficulty,' replied McCready. 'I don't believe they would do anythin' stupid like kill me or Mick, but if they suddenly took it into their heads to break in, there's

100

not a lot we could do to stop 'em and to be honest, I don't think either of us would attempt to. We could threaten the ringleaders with arrest and a court trial, I suppose.'

'And you think if I was here it might help stop them breaking in?'

'One extra gun, especially a stranger who isn't scared to kill if necessary, might just deter the hotheads among 'em.'

'And neither you nor Mick here would be prepared to kill any of them?' asked Caleb.

'We've known these folk all of our lives,' said McCready. 'Most are friends.'

'But they're not friends of mine,' grinned Caleb. 'What do you think would happen to me if I was to kill one of them? I'll tell you what would happen, I'd be swinging on a rope alongside those three in no time at all. No thanks, Mr McCready, I don't like the odds.'

'OK,' nodded McCready, 'I can't say that I blame you. If you don't intend to help, I suggest you go back outside. If they do break in some of them are mean enough to lynch you just because of the colour of your skin.'

'That wouldn't be the first time,' nodded Caleb. 'It just goes to show that I should have brought them in dead.'

'It sure would've saved us a whole heap of trouble,' said Deputy Bywater.

Caleb opened the door of the office and the baying crowd suddenly lapsed into silence as if expecting something, but when it was apparent that nothing was going to happen and Caleb pushed his way through the crowd, they began shouting even louder.

At about one o'clock, Caleb went to the saloon to see if he could get something to eat and noted that the crowd outside the sheriffs office had dwindled to a few, perhaps a dozen, who were still demanding the handing over of the prisoners. These included the Jones brothers.

Although there was no choice of food

in the saloon, the stew that was on offer proved very tasty and, washed down with a beer, Caleb felt very satisfied. He had just finished his meal when the Jones brothers sat themselves down at his table.

'We been thinkin',' declared Jed. 'You remember them papers we found of Pa's back at our place?' Caleb nodded. 'Well, we been to the lawyer an' the bank an' it seems that Pa took out a mortgage on the farm an' still owes three thousand dollars and the bank has given us a month to raise the money. Now, there ain't no way we can get that kinda money together in a month. The most we can hope to raise from our tobacco crop is around two thousand an' we still have to live and rebuild the farm. We got round to thinkin' that it'd be only right if'n you was to pay that three thousand for us.'

Normally, Caleb would have been full of sympathy for someone left in those circumstances and would undoubtedly have helped, but there was something about the brothers Jones which told him not to. There was also something about the deaths of the Jones family which troubled him. He could not put a finger on it, but he had the distinct feeling that things were not quite as they appeared.

'As sorry as I am for what happened,' he replied, 'I see no reason why I should help you since it was me who took all the risks.'

'Told you he wouldn't want to know,' said Aaron to his brother. 'Blacks is all the same, ain't interested in anybody else. Mind you, I would've thought that a minister would've practised what they is allus preachin', love your neighbour an' all that rubbish.'

'I am not your neighbour,' said Caleb, deciding it was time he left. He could feel their eyes boring into his back as he walked to the door and could almost hear just what they were thinking. He knew that he would have to be very careful of those two, especially when he received the reward. The feeling that all was not as it seemed persisted and, seeing that the crowd had now completely dispersed from outside the sheriff's office and, acting purely on an impulse, Caleb went in.

'It looks like they soon got tired,' he said to Sheriff McCready.

'They'll be back,' replied McCready, firmly. 'I ain't never seen 'em like this before. They want blood and they're determined to get it. I hear there's a meetin' been called in the saloon this afternoon.'

'With the Jones boys shouting the loudest I suppose,' said Caleb. 'Actually, Sheriff, it was the Jones brothers I wanted to talk to you about. I don't know why it is, but I have this feeling that what happened at their farm was not as straightforward as it seems. I never really thought about it before and if I had I would have questioned Frank Sullivan a bit closer, but I don't think it was necessarily as the brothers claim. I'd like to question those three, if you don't mind.'

'I don't see that it matters that much what happened,' said McCready. 'The Jones boys say they murdered their parents and their sisters and Sullivan hasn't denied it. That's good enough for me.'

'I'd still like to talk to them,' said Caleb.

'Be my guest,' sighed McCready. 'You'd better do it while you've still got the chance; they could be swingin' on the end of a rope by this time tomorrow.'

'You'd let the mob take them?'

'Let's just say I wouldn't risk my life to stop 'em.' He nodded at a door at the far end of the room. 'The cells are through there. There ain't nobody else in there so you can talk without bein' overheard.'

Caleb nodded his thanks and went through the door where he found the three of them in different cells. They sneered contempt as the preacher entered.

'We heard the mob,' said Frank Sullivan. 'I suppose you is just gonna stand by an' let 'em lynch us.'

'If they decide to break in there isn't much any of us can do about it,' said Caleb. 'Even if the ringleaders are arrested and tried, it won't do you a lot of good if you're dead, will it? Talking of ringleaders, it's them I want to talk to you about.'

'I guess you mean the two boys from that farm,' said Winston Marshall. 'We guessed it was them stirrin' all the others up.'

'Well, you did murder their parents and their sisters and burn down their farm,' Caleb pointed out. 'I'd say they've probably got more cause than most to want to see you kicking your feet on the end of a rope.'

'Not that anyone would believe us,' said Grant Marshall, 'but we never touched their ma an' pa. We didn't even know they was there, not until we come to set fire to the place.'

'I believe you,' said Caleb, not at all surprised by what he heard. 'What about the girls, you did rape and murder them, didn't you?'

'They was still alive when we left!' asserted Frank Sullivan. 'Sure enough, we enjoyed ourselves with 'em, but they was still alive when we rode out. Like Grant says, we didn't even know their ma an' pa was in the house until we set fire to it. We found 'em lyin' at the side of the bed, but by then it was too late to put the fire out.'

'Why didn't you tell me all this before?' asked Caleb.

'What the hell was the point, you wouldn't've believed us?' said Grant. 'We got enough killin's behind us to know we'll end up on the end of a rope no matter what we're arrested for. Who the hell would believe what we say against someone like them brothers?'

'Would it surprise you if I told you that I believed you?' asked Caleb. 'It's true, I do, although I agree that it isn't going to make any difference as to what happens to you. I've had this feeling for a time that something was wrong. It's nothing you've said or done, but more the way those boys acted. It just didn't seem natural.'

'I can't see why you is bothered,' said Frank. 'We is goin' to hang, you'll get your money an' them boys will get away with murderin' their own parents and sisters.'

'Not if I can help it,' said Caleb. 'I know I went after you because of the reward and I make no apologies for that, but I don't like to see anyone blamed for something they didn't do. At least what you tell me explains why they want a lynching; they don't want to chance you saying anything in court.'

'Not that it's goin' to do us any good, but thanks for that,' said Frank.

'Are you quite certain that the parents were dead before you set fire to the place?'

'Nothin' more certain,' said Grant. 'I found 'em both with their throats cut.'

'An' them girls was still alive when we'd

finished with 'em,' asserted Winston.

'And you didn't see the boys?' pressed Caleb.

'Didn't even know there were any,' said Frank. 'I guess we turned up at just the right time to give someone a good alibi.'

'That's certainly how it looks,' nodded Caleb. 'The only trouble is, how do I prove it was the boys who murdered their own family?'

'Why the hell bother?' asked Frank. 'There can't be anythin' in it for you.'

'I just like to have things right,' said Caleb. 'Anyhow, I know it won't help you at all but thanks, although I must say that I have no regrets about bringing you in. I'm glad now that I didn't kill you all, it would have been playing right into the hands of those boys.'

'Glad to be of help!' sneered Frank.

Caleb returned to the front office and Sheriff McCready just as the mob, once again led by the Jones brothers, was gathering again.

'Find out what you wanted?' asked McCready.

'And more,' nodded Caleb. 'Sheriff, I reckon it's now more important than ever that you don't let that mob do a lynching ...' He went on tell the sheriff what he had been told.

FIVE

Sheriff McCready looked disbelievingly at Caleb for a few moments before walking over to the window and thoughtfully gazing out at the crowd and the Jones brothers in particular. Eventually he turned, sighed heavily and seated himself behind his desk.

'I hear what you're sayin', Reverend,' he said quietly. 'Strangely enough I'm inclined to think that Sullivan is tellin' the truth. Don't ask me why I believe him, but it does sort of tie in with certain other things I've been hearin' about them boys, some of it from their pa, Ernie. About three weeks ago, Ernie told me that he's had enough of the pair of them and was goin' to turn 'em out. I don't really know what the trouble was, but I reckon it came down to money and the fact that Jed was apparently messin' about with his sister. I think I told you the rumour was that she had had a baby not long ago, but there was no sign of a baby when I was there and when I did mention it I was more or less laughed off the place by all of them. Ernie said that Jed had threatened to kill him if he did try turnin' him out, but that could easily have been just talk on the spur of the moment.'

'But what they said has put a different light on things?' suggested Caleb. 'I can think of no reason why they should make up such a story. It would make no difference to what happens to them and they know it.'

'It sure does put a different light on things,' admitted McCready. 'The thing is, what the hell can I do about it? Any average lawyer would be able to get those boys off any charge under the circumstances. The thing that puzzles me is why kill their sisters? That don't make sense.'

'As I see it,' interrupted Deputy Bywater, 'it makes perfect sense.' McCready looked at his deputy with some surprise. 'The girls must've known what happened to their ma an' pa,' the deputy continued. 'I knew the younger one, Martha, fairly well, well enough to know that she hated her brothers and that she would've told you. I don't know about the older sister, Kate, especially since she appears to have been ... er ... with her brother.'

Sheriff McCready nodded and glanced towards the window. 'I guess we ought to have them in and tackle 'em about it,' he said.

'You have no evidence,' Caleb pointed out. 'I'm not trying to tell you how to do your job, but for the moment I believe that if they are allowed to think they have got away with it, we just might be able to force their hand.'

'It certainly explains just why they're so hell-fire bent on a lynchin',' nodded McCready. 'I hear the bank is callin' in a loan Ernie had. I can't see them boys raisin' that kind of money though. But that's somethin' between them an' the bank; it's no concern of mine.'

'They've already suggested that I should pay it out of the reward,' Caleb grinned.

'And are you?'

'No chance!' he laughed.

'I suppose we could try to persuade Frank Sullivan to testify in court,' said McCready. 'I don't really see that workin' though. Like I say, any average lawyer straight out of law school would be able to rip their evidence to pieces. OK, I'll go along with lettin' 'em think they've got away with it for the time bein', especially since it looks like I don't have any choice.' He turned to his deputy. 'I don't want one word of this gettin' out to anyone.'

'Sure thing,' agreed Mick Bywater.

The following morning, Sheriff McCready was called out to one of the more remote farms, leaving Deputy Mick Bywater in sole charge. The sheriff said that he would try to get back by nightfall, but there was no guarantee that he would be able to. His instruction to his deputy was that he was to ignore anything else that might occur in the town and ensure that the mob did not attack the jail, but if they did, he was not to place himself in unnecessary danger. He also asked Caleb to keep an eye on the situation, although he stressed that he was not giving him permission to assume control, Mick Bywater was in charge and would make any necessary decisions.

The word that the sheriff had left town spread rapidly and less than half an hour after the sheriff had departed, the mob outside the office appeared larger than ever and were certainly more vocal in their demands. This time, Jed Jones had produced a rope tied in a noose which he waved about, inciting the mob even further.

Caleb watched from a safe distance for some time but eventually he realized that the mob wanted only one thing—blood. Fearing more for Deputy Bywater than the outlaws, he took his guns from their hiding place and, making sure that everyone could see that he was well armed, pushed his way through the crowd and persuaded Mick Bywater to let him in.

'What are you going to do?' Caleb asked.

'Do?' replied the deputy. 'What the hell can I do except sit here an' hope that it's all talk?'

'The way they're acting right now I'd say it was rather more than talk,' said Caleb. 'I've never seen a crowd so heated before.'

'That's because nothin' like this has ever happened before,' said Bywater. 'Most of these farmers have been here all their lives and, generally speakin', they're a law-abidin' lot. Oh, yes, there's the usual messin' about between wives an' men who ain't their husbands, but that usually gets resolved; but somethin' like this unites everyone and most of 'em are still livin' in the past when it comes to justice, they want it quick an' certain.'

'And the normal process of law is not quick enough?'

'Someone told 'em that other places had first claim,' said the deputy. 'As far as they're concerned nobody has better claim than they have, and I must say that my sympathies are with them, or would be if I didn't know that Sullivan and his men didn't murder the Joneses.'

'Then perhaps we should tell them?' suggested Caleb.

'It might make most of 'em think again,' nodded the deputy, 'but that's a decision I'm not prepared to make. Anyhow, it was you who suggested that we didn't tell 'em, somethin' about lettin' Aaron an' Jed think they'd got away with it.'

Caleb nodded and looked out of the window. 'I still think that would be the best way, but it isn't really any concern of mine. All I want is my money and to get out of here.'

'And leave us to clear up the mess,' shrugged Bywater. 'I guess you're right, it ain't your concern.'

The mob was becoming increasingly restless although most still appeared very reluctant to storm the jail, perhaps due to a natural fear of breaking the law but, more likely, Caleb thought, the prospect of facing both himself and Deputy Bywater. As Caleb looked out of the window, a well-dressed man suddenly pushed his way through the crowd and hammered on the office door.

'You've got a visitor,' Caleb said to the deputy.

'It's the mayor,' said Bywater, peering through the glass. 'He's been out of town and we weren't expectin' him back until tomorrow. I'd better let him in.' He unlocked the door and the mayor slipped breathlessly inside.

'What the hell is going on?' he demanded, looking warily at Caleb. 'Where's

Mr McCready?'

'He's had to go out to the Spellman place at Pine Ridge,' explained Bywater. 'There's been some cattle stolen.'

'Then kindly explain just what is going on here,' said the mayor. 'I have heard some garbled story about the Joneses out at Yermo Creek being murdered and some preacher catching those responsible.' He looked hard at Caleb.

'The Reverend Caleb Black, at your service.' Caleb grinned, raising his hat slightly. 'What you have heard is basically correct,' he added. 'The only two survivors from the Jones farm are the boys, Jed and Aaron, and I am responsible for bringing the outlaws to justice.'

'A well-armed preacher as well,' sniffed the mayor, eyeing Caleb up and down.

'Mr Black is also a bounty hunter,' explained Mick Bywater. 'We're waitin' for someone to come from the governor's office to identify the outlaws and to give clearance for the reward.'

'And how much will that be?' the mayor sniffed again.

'Five thousand five hundred dollars,' said Caleb.

'I see,' grunted the mayor. 'And who, exactly, is worth that much money?'

Deputy Bywater produced the four Wanted posters which the mayor examined briefly.

'That makes you a very rich man, Reverend. Perhaps I had better introduce myself. Clifford Sanderson, known to most as Sandy. Where are these men now?'

'Where else but in the jail?' said Caleb.

'I want to see them,' ordered the mayor, glaring at Deputy Bywater who was plainly ill at ease but agreed to the mayor going through to the cells. 'There's only three of them,' he said when he returned, not having spoken to the men at all. 'Where is the other one?'

'In a box at the undertaker's,' said Caleb. 'I killed him.'

Once again Mayor Sanderson looked

Caleb up and down. 'Then those guns are not just for show,' he remarked. 'Is it normal for a minister to go round killing people, even outlaws and murderers?'

'It's normal for this particular preacher,' Caleb grinned. 'Now, as you can see, Mr Mayor, that crowd out there don't seem to agree that those men should be handed over to whoever comes from the governor's office. It would appear that they want a more instant solution.'

'That's understandable,' said the mayor. 'Although I agree that we must not let mob-rule dictate things.'

'Then I suggest that you use your position as mayor to order them to disperse,' said Caleb.

'I think we ought to tell the mayor what we know about what happened at the Jones farm,' suggested Mick Bywater.

'I think I ought to be in possession of all the facts,' said the mayor. 'I don't want to stand out there and make a fool of myself.'

'Those men in the jail didn't murder any of the Joneses,' said Caleb.

The mayor looked hard at the preacher for a moment. 'Then who did?' he finally demanded.

'Jed and Aaron,' said Bywater.

'If I heard you right,' said the mayor. 'You claim those two boys murdered their own parents and their sisters. If that is the case, why are they not also locked up in the jail?'

'Because we do not have any proof,' explained Caleb. 'All we have is the word of three wanted outlaws that it was not they who murdered the family.' He went on to explain.

'Obviously they are trying to shift the blame,' said the mayor. 'Who would ever believe that story? I'm surprised that either of you give any credence to it, although I suppose in your case, Mr Black, it is understandable.'

'By that I take it you mean it is understandable because I am a Negro like they are?' said Caleb. 'Mr Mayor, let me assure you that neither the colour of their skin nor my own has anything to do with it. It won't benefit Sullivan to spread rumours like that, they're going to end up on the end of the hangman's rope no matter what. There was something about the way those boys acted when I first met them—I was there just after the outlaws had left—which just wasn't natural. I believe Sullivan.'

'Then question them!'

'That would achieve precisely nothing,' said Caleb. 'Any average lawyer would soon discredit the testimony of three desperate outlaws.'

The mayor thought for a moment. 'You're right,' he eventually acknowledged. 'I am a lawyer, I ought to know. So, how do we prove the Jones boys did murder their own parents and sisters?'

'That's your problem,' Caleb grinned. 'As soon as my money is through I shall be on my way. In the meantime, I think it is important that someone gets that crowd to see some sense. The only reason the Jones boys want a lynching is to stop Sullivan saying what he has in a court of law.'

'Then we tell them,' said the mayor. 'That should quieten them down.'

'Or it could make them more determined,' said Mick Bywater. 'It's one thing for Sullivan to make a claim that could be easily passed off as desperate men looking for desperate solutions, but the last thing they would want is such a thing being said in court, under oath.'

'I couldn't have put it better myself,' said Caleb. 'In the meantime I think you should go out there and try to instil some sense into them.'

Mayor Sanderson drew a deep breath, straightened his cravat, fastened the top button of his jacket, coughed nervously and went to the door. 'This really is a job for Mr McCready,' he said. 'However, since he isn't here and I doubt if anyone would take Mick too seriously, I suppose the task must fall to me. Very well, but I cannot promise anything you understand.' He opened the door slightly and then turned to Caleb and the deputy again. 'You be ready to take whatever action is necessary.' Caleb did not believe that any action on their part would be necessary. The mayor went outside and stood on the boardwalk, which raised him above the crowd.

Very slowly, as the mayor raised his arms and waved his hands in an attempt to quieten them down, the crowd responded and eventually all were staring, waiting expectantly.

The silence was broken by Jed Jones suddenly shouting and waving the rope. 'Are you goin' to hand 'em over?' he demanded, a demand which brought a ripple of approval from the others.

'My friends!' said the mayor, huskily. 'I fully realize how you must feel, and believe me, my sympathies are entirely with Jed and Aaron. However, for many years now this town has prided itself in the fact that the rule of law has always been upheld and this case is no different ...'

'Murder is a hangin' offence!' called one of the crowd. 'That's the law an' all we want is to see justice carried out.'

'And justice will be carried out,' replied the mayor, 'but not the kind of justice to which you refer. Lynching is a thing of the past; these days we have proper laws and courts to deal with such matters ...'

'Then let's have us a court right here!' shouted Jed Jones. 'You can be the judge, you are a lawyer, then when they've been found guilty we can string 'em up from that tree over there.' He pointed to a large tree at the end of the street.

'I am not a judge,' croaked the mayor. 'I am not empowered to sit in such a capacity.'

'We just made you a judge!' shouted another voice. 'Ain't that right?' he called to the crowd. There was a roar of approval followed by more demands for instant justice.

'Quite impossible!' shouted the mayor, trying to make himself heard above the noise. 'The normal process of law must be adhered to.'

'I hear they're to be taken away from here,' called Aaron Jones. 'Somethin' about them bein' wanted in other places.'

'That may well be the case,' said the mayor. 'That decision is entirely up to the state legal department. The thing is, wherever they are tried, it is almost certain that they will be sentenced to death.'

'Then let's do it here!' shouted Jed Jones. 'It'd sure save a whole lot of money an' time-wastin'.'

'My friends,' said the mayor, once again attempting to quieten them down. 'I'm sorry, I cannot allow such a thing to happen. After all, it is just possible that these men are not guilty of the murders.'

'You wasn't there!' shouted Jed. 'Me an' Aaron saw the whole thing, so don't go tellin' us that they might not have done it.'

'True, I wasn't there,' agreed the mayor, 'but even if there were other witnesses, I could not allow a lynching to take place.'

'Are you callin' me an' Aaron liars?' demanded Jed. The crowd suddenly surged forward a few yards and Mayor Sanderson stepped back, nervously feeling for the door handle.

'I am not calling anyone a liar,' he croaked. 'All I am saying is that mistakes have been made in the past.'

'Which is the same as callin' me an' Aaron liars!' shouted Jed. 'You got ten minutes to hand 'em over,' he continued. 'After that we might just take 'em ourselves so don't say you ain't been warned.'

'You would be very foolish to take such a course of action,' said the mayor, his hand finding the door handle and turning it. 'I must warn you that any attempt to take those men by force will be met by force and some of you are liable to get hurt, possibly even killed.' He opened the door and slipped inside the office to boos and calls for him to stand down as town mayor.

'I guess you did your best,' said Caleb. 'I don't think it did much good though.' He checked that both his handguns were loaded and advised Mick Bywater to do the same.

'If they come, they come,' said the deputy. 'I don't intend drawin' my gun against any one of them. Scum like Sullivan just ain't worth it.'

'That goes for me too,' said the mayor. 'Besides, I don't think I could ever shoot any man, especially men with whom I have lived and worked most of my life.'

'Then I reckon the best thing I can do is make myself scarce,' nodded Caleb. 'The mood they are in at this moment, they are liable to turn on me just because of the colour of my skin. The difference is that I am not afraid to use my guns if I have to and if they do turn against me, they're likely to find that out. Whatever happens now is your problem, you can count me out. As far as I am concerned I have done my duty in bringing those men in and I am entitled to that reward.'

'You'll get your money,' grunted out Mayor Sanderson. 'I don't think anyone would deny you your right to it. The problem as far as I see it is that if that crowd out there know you're not here, they'll be more likely to storm the place.'

'Not my problem,' replied Caleb very firmly. 'I'll leave you to it. I only hope that nobody gets injured.' Without another word he opened the door and stepped outside.

His sudden appearance caused the crowd to stop shouting and talking and all stared hard as if expecting the preacher to make a statement. When he did not and pushed his way through, a few made comments about all Negroes being the same and accusing Caleb of being in league with the outlaws. Caleb chose to ignore them, he was used to such comments.

'Someone ought to ride out to the Spellman place and tell Mr McCready just what is going on here,' suggested Deputy Bywater as he watched Caleb push his way through the crowd.

'I agree,' said the mayor. 'The problem is who? It seems to me that almost everyone in town is involved in this thing; I don't think we could rely on anyone.'

'There must be someone,' said the deputy. 'If there isn't I suppose I had better go out there myself.'

'You'll remain here!' ordered the mayor. 'You might be needed. Leave it to me, I have a couple of ideas. Will you be all right on your own?'

'I guess so,' nodded Mick. 'If they do come in, I won't stop them.'

'Don't tell them that,' urged the mayor. 'I'll go and see what I can do about getting the sheriff back here.' Once again silence descended as he stepped on to the boardwalk.

'Changed your mind?' came the call.

'About handing them over?' replied the mayor. 'No. They remain where they are, in jail.' He was tempted to tell them that he was sending for Sheriff McCready, but decided against it, fearing that it might just precipitate action. It was well known that Sheriff McCready was not a man to be intimidated and would not be afraid to shoot if necessary and if they thought he was coming back they might just carry out the threat of lynching the outlaws.

However, as much as Jed and Aaron Jones tried to incite the rest of the crowd, it appeared that interest and support was beginning to ebb and people started to drift away, claiming that they had other things to do, which was probably largely true. The women, those few who were in the crowd, seemed to be the first to lose interest and were, for the most part, closely followed by their menfolk. Eventually, apart from a few older men who seemed to have nothing better to do, there was only a hardcore of

133

younger, unattached men backing Jed and Aaron and even that backing started to show cracks when Jed Jones tried to incite them to storm the jail.

Inside the sheriff's office, Deputy Mick Bywater breathed a sigh of relief as he watched the crowd which at one point had numbered at least 300, gradually dwindle to exactly eighteen. A short time later, Mayor Sanderson returned to the office with the news that he had been able to persuade someone to ride out to Pine Ridge, news which came as a relief to Mick Bywater. Despite the immediate danger being past, he knew he was out of his depth and felt that the situation needed his superior's attention.

From the porch in front of the hotel, Caleb, too, noted that the danger appeared to have passed, especially when even Jed and Aaron Jones seemed to give up and headed for the saloon. However, he did not really believe that either of the brothers was prepared to let things simply fade away; he knew that they would still try to silence the outlaws if they possibly could.

Half an hour later, Caleb also found himself in the saloon standing alongside Jed and Aaron, both of whom chose to ignore him at first, which suited Caleb, but that situation did not last very long as Jed thrust an empty glass in front of him.

'I figure you owe us a drink at least,' he rasped. 'You is a very rich man now.'

'I haven't been paid yet,' said Caleb. 'I can assure you that if I had been I certainly would not be in Bullhead now.'

'We noticed you chickened out,' grinned Aaron, also thrusting an empty glass in front of Caleb. 'Scared to stay with Mick Bywater just in case.'

Caleb pushed the glass to one side and sneered at Aaron. 'I wouldn't have thought you were old enough to drink,' he said. 'As for chickening out as you put it, it is none of my business, that's all.' He looked both boys up and down. 'I wouldn't have thought that either of you was old enough to do lots of things, but I have heard of kids killing their parents before now.'

Jed and Aaron looked at each other in alarm for a few seconds before Jed replied hoarsely: 'I wouldn't go round makin' accusations like that if'n I was you, Mr Preacherman. You was there, you saw what they did.'

'I saw four dead bodies,' said Caleb. 'I have no idea how they really died or who killed them; I have only your word for what happened.'

'Meanin' what?' demanded Jed.

'Meaning whatever you want it to mean,' grinned Caleb, deciding that it might force the brothers into some form of action if he made it known what he had been told. 'It's just that those outlaws maintain that your mother and father were already dead—their throats cut apparently—and that although they admit they did rape your sisters, they were still alive when they left. Of course, I suppose that men like that will say anything to get off a charge of murder.'

'Too damned right they would,' growled Jed. 'Just don't go round sayin' things like that to nobody; somebody might just believe you.'

'And it would never do for anyone to know the truth,' said Caleb.

Jed nudged his brother and both went off, muttering between themselves, to a corner table where five other youths appeared to be sharing a single drink and two cheroots. Caleb, however, was not happy with the situation, even though it was strictly not his problem. He had told the brothers what the outlaws had claimed, partly to see what reaction he got and partly to plant seeds of doubt in the boys' minds and force them into doing something. He knew that he had succeeded and from that point onwards he would be ready for anything.

SIX

Nothing much happened for the remainder of the day except that Jed and Aaron Jones continued to make it plain to anyone who would listen that they still expected their own form of justice. Whilst initial feelings had been very much on the side of the brothers, there was now a very definite coolness and support was largely confined to a few youths of about their own ages and even these balked at the suggestion that they should storm the jail.

There seemed little doubt that a large part of the cooling of support was due to the rumour about Jed's relationship with his sister, and the baby, which was now beginning to circulate freely, although nobody seemed quite sure who had started it. The farmers might have been behind the boys regarding the murder of their parents and sisters, but the questions raised by the rumours of incest overrode anything else. The farmers were, in essence, a deeply religious group and very conservative in their outlook. They could forgive most things, including infidelity, but not any question of a sexual relationship between brother and sister. The result was that as the rumour spread, sympathy and support for their cause rapidly decreased. It surprised Deputy Bywater that nobody had heard about it before. As was normal under such circumstances, there were a great many who claimed that they had had their suspicions all along.

When Sheriff McCready had not returned by nine o'clock that evening, it was assumed that he would not do so until the following morning at the earliest, an observation which was not lost on the Jones brothers and their few allies. The last time Caleb saw them, they were huddled together, obviously planning something.

Although trying to convince himself that whatever they planned to do was none of his business, Caleb somehow felt duty bound to make it his business and he spent some time quietly patrolling the town.

At just after ten o'clock, Deputy Mick Bywater checked on his prisoners before making himself as comfortable as he could in the office for the night. Everything appeared normal; two of the three seemed to be asleep and the third, Winston Marshall, was lounging on his bunk staring at the ceiling. No words passed between them and Mick returned to the office.

Inside the jail, Winston Marshall suddenly looked up at the small, barred, glassless window high above his head and listened intently. There it was again, a definite 'Pssst' as if someone was trying to attract his attention. Very slowly he rose, glanced briefly at the adjoining door to the office and then stood on his bunk.

He was just tall enough to look through the window.

'You want outa there?' whispered a voice.

'What do you think?' Winston whispered in reply.

'Here, take these,' whispered the voice again. 'They is loaded.'

Before Winston could say anything the butt of a handgun was thrust through the bars. He looked slightly alarmed, but snatched the weapon which was immediately followed by another and then another.

'Who the hell are you?' hissed Winston. 'What you doin' this for?'

'Let's just say I'm a friend,' came the reply. 'All you've got to do now is get that deputy in there an' take his keys. Your horses are in the paddock behind the jail, ready to ride.'

By that time the other two had woken up and Winston hissed at them to be quiet. His further questions to whoever was outside were met by silence. Slowly he climbed off his bunk, clutching the guns and, in the dim light, showed them to the others.

'It's a trick!' whispered Frank Sullivan. 'Why the hell would anyone want to help us? I don't like it.'

'Maybe you'd prefer swingin' on the end of a rope,' said Winston. 'OK, so it's a trick, but these guns are loaded, just like the man said. Even if it is a trick, it means we have some sort of chance of gettin' out of here alive. Here, take one an' pass the other to Grant.' He pushed two of the guns through the bars and Frank handed one on to Grant in the other cell. All three once again checked that they were loaded with real bullets and not blanks.

'So what do we do now?' asked Grant. 'Frank's right, nobody ain't goin' to help us out of the goodness of their heart.'

'Whoever it was reckoned our horses are saddled in the paddock,' said Winston. 'I can't see nothin' from here. How about you, Grant, you've got a window overlookin' the back?'

Grant stood on his bunk, but could not see through the window. After pulling himself up by gripping the bars, he eventually confirmed that he thought he could see three saddled horses in the paddock.

'It's the best chance we've got,' said Grant. 'In fact it's just about the only chance we've got. Trick or no trick, I'm all for givin' it a try.'

'Me too,' confirmed Winston. Frank still appeared rather uncertain.

'We go for it!' Frank suddenly decided. 'Get that deputy in here.'

Whilst he was wandering around the town, Caleb found himself at the livery stable and, with little else to do, he went inside to check on his horse. She appeared contented enough and after giving her a few more oats, he turned to leave. However, at the door he suddenly stopped and looked back.

Although the light was very dim, something did not seem right to him and he had long since learned to trust his feelings on such matters. He took a few steps back into the building and stood for a while looking around but nothing struck him as being out of place although the feeling that something was not as it ought to be persisted.

It was not the absence of horses; there had been three of them in the stalls earlier that day and there were still three of them now. It did not appear that anyone had been in there and everything appeared as he would have expected in any livery. He returned to the door, opened it and stepped out but the feeling would not leave him and he was forced to return and once again look around.

He must have been standing there for about five minutes before it suddenly hit him what was wrong. When he had brought the outlaws into town, their horses had been taken to the livery where they had been unsaddled before being turned out

144

into a paddock behind the livery. The saddles had been placed over a partition, all four of them in a line. He took a few steps to the partition and realized that there was now only one saddle. His mind immediately leapt to the obvious conclusion that if three of the saddles were missing, three of the horses would also have disappeared. A quick check in the paddock confirmed this, since he knew that earlier that day there had been four horses—now there was only one.

At first, Caleb wondered if, for some reason, both saddles and horses had been removed to somewhere else, but he discarded this idea because there was no obvious reason for such a move. His second thought was that someone had stolen them and this was still a possibility, although it seemed most unlikely since both horses and saddles of the quality of those belonging to the outlaws were very rare amongst farmers. The only people with that quality of animal would be the few ranchers and he doubted very much if any rancher would stoop to stealing, especially direct from the livery.

There was a voice and the sudden glare of an oil lamp behind him, the voice demanding to know who was there. Caleb turned to assure the livery owner that he was just looking at his horse.

'I thought I heard someone round here about half an hour ago,' said Jack Spate, the owner. 'I didn't see nothin' though. Most likely it was just some kids.'

'Didn't you notice anything then?' asked Caleb.

'Such as?'

'Take a look around now,' said Caleb. 'What do you see?'

'Nothin',' replied Jack Spate. 'What am I supposed to see?'

'Take another look in the paddock,' said Caleb.

'I see a horse. So what?'

'Exactly,' said Caleb. 'You see a horse. Now, come on inside and tell me what you see.' Rather bewildered, Jack followed

Caleb inside and, with the glow of the oil lamp to help him, gazed around for a few moments.

'OK, Mr Black, I give up. If this is some kind of game, you win,' he said.

'How many horses should there have been in the paddock?' Caleb asked.

'Four; the ones belongin' to ... Oh yeah, I see what you're gettin' at,' said Jack. 'There's only one now.' He looked about the livery again. 'They're gone too, three saddles. There was four of 'em over there, now there's only one. What the hell's goin' on, Mr Black?'

'I was rather hoping that you would be able to tell me,' said Caleb. 'So, as far as you're concerned, there should be four horses and four saddles. Nobody said anything to you about moving them?'

'Not a word,' confirmed Jack. 'I ain't got nobody stayin' in the bunkhouse either. In fact, apart from you there ain't no strangers in town right now.'

'Does it have to be strangers?' asked Caleb.

'Who else?' asked Jack.

'Indeed, who else?' sighed Caleb. 'More importantly, why?'

'On account they needed 'em,' replied Jack with simple logic. 'I ain't much good at thinkin, but it seems to me that someone took 'em 'cos they wanted 'em pretty bad. The only thing is, animals like that'd be too easy to trace if one of the farmers took 'em, an' they'd know that.'

'The question is, who would need them?' Caleb said, more to himself than Jack Spate. 'I reckon I'd better go and tell Deputy Bywater what has happened. It is just possible that he knows something about it, although I should have thought he would have told you.'

'He never said nothin' to me,' said Jack. 'There's another thing; there's three sets of bridles an' bits missin', so whoever took 'em is intendin' to ride somewhere.' Caleb had not noticed the absence of bridles and bits, especially as there were quite a few sets hanging on the walls.

'I'm going to tell the deputy,' said Caleb.

The streets of Bullhead were very quiet, most of the farmers having long since returned home and the residents of the town for the most part having retired. The only sign of life came from the saloon in the form of the occasional shout and the strains of a tune being forced from the out-of-tune piano. It was the very absence of people and other sounds which made Caleb peer along the street in the direction of the sheriffs office and jail.

If asked to swear on oath that he had either seen or heard something, he could not have done so, but he was quite convinced that he had seen shadows flitting between buildings, obviously attempting to keep out of sight. To his mind, anyone intent on keeping out of sight at any time of the night was up to no good.

He slipped up an alley intending to go to the sheriff's office along the backs of the houses and stores in the hope of seeing the figures again. He did not see or hear anyone, but the sight of three, saddled horses in the paddock behind the jail confirmed to him that something was very wrong and his immediate thought was for the safety of Deputy Sheriff Mick Bywater ...

'Sheriff!' called Frank Sullivan. 'Sheriff,' he called again. 'You come on in here, we got somethin' to tell you.'

Mick Bywater had been asleep and at first he thought he had been dreaming, but when the call came again, this time louder, he grudgingly eased himself out of the leather chair in which he had managed to make himself comfortable, stretched and yawned, checked what time it was, discovered that it was almost 11.30 and cursed as Frank Sullivan called out yet again.

'I'm comin'!' he yelled back. 'You just wait, you ain't goin' nowhere.' However, before he could do anything else, a knock came on the door. Once again, Mick cursed, but decided that he had better see who it was, hoping that it was not someone from the saloon saying that there was trouble. He unlocked the door and looked bleary-eyed at Caleb. 'Mr Black,' he said. 'What the hell are you doin' here at this time of night?'

'I might be wrong,' said Caleb, pushing his way in, 'and I hope I am, but I think you've got some trouble coming.'

'Trouble is somethin' I can do without,' said Mick. 'What kind of trouble?'

'That I don't know,' said Caleb. 'There's three horses and three saddles missing from the livery and now those same three horses are standin' in the paddock at the back of the jail. One thing is certain, they didn't get there by themselves.' Mick's reply was interrupted by yet another call from the prisoners. Caleb immediately motioned to

151

Mick that he was not to let on that he had arrived.

'I'm comin'!' shouted Mick. 'You just hang on in there.'

Caleb immediately took up a position behind the door leading to the jail, drew his gun and then nodded to the deputy. Mick opened the door and went through to the cells.

'Now don't you go doin' nothin' stupid,' hissed Winston Marshall from the first cell, as he thrust a gun into Mick's neck and grabbed the deputy's arm through the bars. 'This gun is loaded an' all it needs is for me to squeeze this trigger for you to be a very dead sheriff. We've all got guns, so you just do as you're told.'

'Your keys,' ordered Frank Sullivan. 'Unlock these cages an' let us outa here an' you might not get hurt. We ain't never killed a lawman yet but there's always a first time.'

'They're in the desk,' winced Mick, as his arm was bent through the bars.

'Search him!' hissed Sullivan.

'No need to,' grated Caleb from behind the door, 'he's telling the truth. You don't think he'd be stupid enough to carry them with him, do you?'

'Black!' snarled Sullivan. 'Well, now it's you what's bein' stupid. You go fetch them keys or else he gets a hole blown in his head.'

'Now who's being stupid?' Caleb replied. 'That's one sure way for all three of you to end up dead. Believe me, nobody would shed any tears if I did kill you and the fact that you have somehow got hold of guns gives me the perfect excuse.'

'We mean it!' hissed Winston Marshall. 'We is for the rope anyhow, so killin' the deputy here ain't goin' to make no difference. If you do shoot us it'd just mean we die that bit earlier.'

'The keys!' insisted Frank Sullivan. 'That way him an' you both get to live an' we get the chance to get away.'

'I don't know how you got hold of those

guns,' said Caleb, 'but it's obvious that you had outside help and I think I can guess where that help came from. Doesn't it strike you that someone wants you to escape just so that they can kill you and then take the credit?'

'Sure,' laughed Frank. 'We know it's a set up, but it's the best chance we have of gettin' out of here. Now, Reveren', those keys. I can assure you that we have absolutely nothin' to lose; we is dead men for sure if we don't take this chance. Once we're outside it's just possible that things could go our way. Those keys, Reveren'.'

Caleb thought for a moment; they were quite right, they did indeed have nothing to lose and had everything to gain. He realized that they were desperate enough to carry out their threat and he knew that he could not take the risk of Mick Bywater being killed.

'Do as they say!' ordered the deputy. 'Scum like them just ain't worth me gettin' killed for. Mr McCready told me that I wasn't to take any risks with my life. If they get out an' then get killed by the Jones brothers, it'll save everyone a whole lot of trouble.'

'And ruin any chance you might have of proving that Jed and Aaron murdered their mother and father,' reminded Caleb.

'Right now I don't give a shit about that,' winced Mick, as his arm was given a sudden twist. 'I just don't want to die for either the Jones boys or these three.'

'OK,' sighed Caleb, 'but I shall still expect my money; it won't be my fault if they get away. I'll go get the keys. Where are they?'

'Top right-hand drawer.' Mick winced again. 'The bunch with eight keys.'

'Now you're talkin' sense,' laughed Frank Sullivan. 'Don't you go tryin' nothin' stupid though, Reveren', we ain't never killed a preacher yet either, but I guess there's always a first time for everythin' an' I guess it won't make no difference as to where we end up when we're dead, we've already booked our place in hell.'

'You just throw them guns of yours inside here,' ordered Winston Marshall.

'No deal!' replied Caleb, firmly. 'I give you the keys and then you take your chance as to what happens.'

'Your guns!' barked Winston.

'No!' said Caleb. 'I keep my guns and you get the keys or, if you like, you kill the deputy and then I kill you.'

'The keys!' interrupted Frank Sullivan. 'We can use the deputy as cover.'

'I'll go along with that,' agreed Caleb. 'OK, I'm going for the keys.' He went to the desk, found the bunch of eight and returned to the door. 'OK, I've got them,' he said. 'What now?'

'You just make sure you ain't got a gun in your hand,' said Frank. 'Open the door an' throw the keys into the first cell. And don't think you can get the deputy out before we unlock these cages. He's bein' handed on to me so Winston's hands are

156

free an' one false move from you means the end of him. You got that?'

'Loud and clear,' confirmed Caleb. Slowly he opened the door and, in the dim light issuing from the office, could see that the situation was exactly as the men had said. Mick Bywater was now held by Frank Sullivan, the gun firmly placed against his temple. Caleb lobbed the keys but they hit the bars and clattered to the floor, just out of reach of Winston's long arms.

'Pick 'em up!' ordered Winston. 'This time you hand 'em to me.' Caleb did as he was ordered and this time Winston snatched the keys. 'Which one is which?' he grated at Mick Bywater.

'They're numbered,' said Mick. 'Yours is number one, the others are two and three. The others are for the other three cells, the front and the back door.' 'Which one's the front door?' Winston demanded again, fumbling through the bunch and peering at each key.

'It has a "B" stamped on it,' said Mick.

Winston eventually found the key to his cell and, after two attempts, managed to insert the key and open the door. He growled at Caleb who was now standing just inside the door and then fumbled through the keys again until he found those marked '2' and '3' and then released his companions.

For a few moments, Frank Sullivan stared hard at Caleb, the gun in his hand wavering slightly as his fingers twitched. Suddenly he smiled and then laughed.

'In here, the two of you,' he said. 'I was thinkin' about killin' you, Reveren', but I won't, not unless we meet again.' He pushed Mick Bywater into the cell and stood aside as Caleb also went inside. Surprisingly, Caleb thought, nobody made any attempt to take his guns. 'That should keep you quiet for a time. Have you ever been in jail before, Reveren'?'

'Once,' admitted Caleb. 'You are riding

into a trap, you know that, don't you?'

'We is prepared to take that chance,' hissed Grant Marshall.

Frank Sullivan slammed the cell door and locked it. He then found the key to the back door and the three left Caleb and Mick, locking the door through to the cells behind them. They heard the back door of the office being opened followed by whispered instructions which neither of them could make out. For a few minutes there was silence and Caleb assumed that far from simply taking the horses and attempting to ride out, the outlaws were being very cautious and checking out where the Jones brothers were likely to be.

After a time, perhaps ten minutes, the unmistakeable sounds of horses being mounted and ridden away were suddenly followed by shouting and shooting ...

As soon as they were outside, Frank Sullivan held the other two back and nodded that each should go a different way. There was no need for any verbal instruction. Ten minutes later they reassembled by the back door.

'There's three of 'em down the alley just along the street,' said Grant. 'They didn't see me though.'

'An' there's another three lyin' under the boardwalk between here an' the saloon,' said Winston. 'An' I wouldn't be sure, but I think there's another two hidin' behind a water trough opposite the saloon.'

'An' I'm pretty damned sure there's at least two of 'em on the roof of that corn an' feed merchant's the other way,' said Frank.

'Then it looks like they got all ways out covered,' said Winston. 'What do we do, make a run for it and take the chance?'

'Naw!' said Frank. 'I say we cut across behind the saloon. There's a jumble of houses an' buildin's, but nothin' we can't cope with. We know where most of 'em are, we'll just have to take the chance on there bein' any more.'

'Then let's go!' said Grant.

They opened the gate to the paddock, mounted the horses, and suddenly urged them through a narrow opening which led to the rear of the buildings along the main street. They had gone about fifty yards when there was a shout followed by gunfire.

SEVEN

It was a good ten minutes before anyone came into the sheriff's office and a further two or three minutes and shouts from Caleb and Mick Bywater before the key to the door through to the cells was found. The first person through the door was the mayor, Sandy Sanderson, followed by two others. Eventually, Caleb and the deputy were freed and immediately faced a barrage of questions from the mayor.

'Don't ask me how,' said Mick Bywater, 'but they somehow got hold of some guns an' the only way they could've got them is from the outside.'

'And my money would be on the Jones brothers,' added Caleb.

'Aaron and Jed!' exclaimed the mayor. 'Why should they want to help them to escape? They were the ones howling for blood.'

'Precisely because they wanted them dead,' said Caleb. 'They gave the guns to the outlaws in the hope that they would escape and then they could ambush them, making sure that they were killed. That way they get what they want and end up being hailed as heroes. To my mind, nothing else makes any sense.'

'Well, if that was the case, it would appear that they failed,' muttered the mayor.

'From what I have seen and heard of the Jones boys, it's not at all surprising that they made a mess of things,' said Caleb.

'Where the hell has McCready got to?' grunted the mayor. 'This would never have happened if he had been where he was supposed to be.'

'Cattle stealing is also his business,' said Mick in defence of his senior. 'He's not just sheriff of Bullhead, he has a big area to cover.'

'Mmm ... maybe so,' conceded the mayor. 'But with such important outlaws in his jail he should never have left his deputy in charge, you should have gone to see about the missing cows.'

'I just do what I'm told,' replied Mick. 'Anyway, it's happened now and we have to go after them. I must say that I agree with Mr Black that it must have been the Jones brothers who helped them. I heard some shooting, was anyone hit?'

'Not that I am aware of,' grunted the mayor. 'I don't even know who was shooting at who.'

'Are the Jones brothers in town?' asked Caleb.

'How would I know that?' objected the mayor. He turned to one of the other men with him. 'Sam, you go and see if you can find them.' Sam nodded and left the office. 'In the meantime,' he continued, addressing the deputy, 'since you appear to be in charge, what do you intend doing now?'

'Well, there doesn't seem much point in chasing after them at this time of night,' said Caleb, seeing that Mick appeared rather lost. 'It's bad enough trying to track anyone in daylight, but in the dark it would be impossible.'

'They headed south,' said the other man with the mayor. 'I saw 'em ride out myself.'

'Which doesn't mean a thing,' said Caleb. 'Frank Sullivan is no fool, he'll know that someone saw them and he's quite likely to head off in another direction as soon as he can. I am afraid that you will just have to wait until daylight and hope that you can pick up their trail.'

'Wally Barns!' exclaimed the mayor. 'He used to be a tracker with the army; at least, that's what he claims.' He looked at Caleb. 'Wally is half Indian, he has a farm about three miles out of town.'

'I doubt if even he could follow anyone at night,' smiled Caleb.

'You can always ask him,' said the man

with the mayor. 'He was in the saloon when the shooting started. I'll go get him if you want.'

'Good idea,' agreed the mayor. The man left to find Wally and once again the mayor looked at Caleb. 'Mr Black, I know that you can rightly claim to have done your part in bringing in those outlaws in the first place, but I wonder if the authorities will see it that way. I hope that you will play a full part in going after them.'

'I hadn't intended to,' admitted Caleb. 'It wasn't my fault that you allowed them to escape.'

'*That Deputy Bywater allowed them to escape!*' huffed the mayor. 'Very well, let me put it another way. I am asking you to help. You are a bounty hunter, so you claim, and as such you must be very experienced in tracking and dealing with outlaws. We in Bullhead are definitely not used to such things and we need the help of men like you. Will you help?'

'I'll think about it,' nodded Caleb. 'We

can't start out until the morning, I'll let you know then.'

The man named Sam who had been sent to look for the Jones brothers returned with the not unexpected information that neither of them was to be found and that nobody seemed to know where they were. A short while later, a tall, thin, grizzled-faced man came into the office and looked enquiringly.

'You wanted to see me?' he said.

'Ah, yes,' said the mayor. 'Mr Black, this is Wally Barns, the tracker I was telling you about. Wally, we need your skills and your help. You must know what has happened.'

'Reckon the whole territory must know by now,' replied Wally. 'You want me to follow them outlaws?'

'Yes,' nodded the mayor. 'Mr Black is quite certain that it would be impossible at night. Is it?'

'Not impossible,' said Wally. 'Damned difficult; we'd need torches an' lamps and even then I couldn't guarantee anythin'. It'd be much easier in the mornin'.'

'I'm for leavin' it till the mornin',' said Mick Bywater. 'There don't seem a lot of point in chasin' our tails all night an' endin' up dog tired.'

The mayor thought for a few moments and then nodded. 'Very well, but I want everyone here at first light.'

'Are you ridin' with us?' asked Mick.

The mayor shuffled uneasily. 'I ... er ... er ... No, my place is here in Bullhead. I would if I could, but someone in authority must stay here. I'm quite certain that you will find plenty of willing volunteers.' Caleb had serious doubts.

'I wouldn't like to bet on it,' said Mick, as if in confirmation. 'Mr McCready tried to organize a posse a couple of years ago when there was some cattle rustlin'. The farmers just weren't interested.'

'This is very different,' said the mayor. 'These men are murderers.'

168

Caleb's doubts were confirmed at first light when the only people gathered outside the sheriffs office were himself, Mick Bywater who, as deputy sheriff, was in charge of the party, Wally Barns and the mayor, who was plainly not intending to accompany them. The previous evening, Mick Bywater had tried to recruit a posse and while at the time he had received pledges of support from almost everyone, no one had showed up. Caleb, too, had given serious consideration to any further involvement, but had eventually decided that he had better help, just in case officialdom prevaricated over the payment of his reward.

In the obvious absence of any further volunteers, Mick Bywater, feeling slightly out of his depth, somewhat reluctantly assumed command and led them out of a strangely quiet town. Normally, even at that hour, the store owners were opening up, but not this particular morning: it was almost as if everyone had deliberately overslept in case they should be co-opted into the posse.

Both the mayor and Mick Bywater had expressed doubts as to the ability of Wally Barns, but their fears appeared allayed as only a matter of a few yards along the trail, he suddenly stopped, got off his horse and examined a bush.

'Blood!' he announced. 'Could be one of the horses was hit or it could be one of them. I ain't no expert on which blood is which.'

'There were some shots fired,' said Mick. 'I never did find out just who by.'

Wally studied the ground for a few moments and then grunted, 'I'd say it was one of the horses. Look, up there ...' He pointed further along the track at a dark patch. 'That's blood, too much for a man I'd say. We're lookin' for an injured horse.'

Both Caleb and Mick stared at the dark spot and agreed between themselves that it could have been almost anything as far as they were concerned, but bowed to Wally's apparent greater knowledge. They continued at a fairly leisurely pace along the trail, Wally occasionally stopping to check on a hoof print, a broken twig or a scuff mark. He appeared quite satisfied that they were on the correct road even if Caleb had his doubts, but then he was ready to admit that his tracking abilities were very limited.

'Are there any ways out of this valley?' Caleb asked, looking up at the fairly steep, wooded sides.

'I guess a man could take off anywhere,' answered Mick. 'There ain't no, what you would call, regular roads though.'

'It was just a thought that maybe they had taken to the hills and the forest,' said Caleb. 'Do you think we are still following them?'

'I'd stake my life on them not havin' left this trail yet,' said Wally, obviously resenting what he thought was a slur on his abilities. 'It might've been a long time since I tracked a man, but I sure have tracked enough deer an' wolves since then an' if I can track them I reckon I can track a man on horseback easy enough.' In defence of his claim he pointed at another dark stain on the ground. 'More blood. There's been lots of it all along the road. I reckon we're goin' to find us one dead horse pretty soon now.'

They came upon a farm and Mick decided that he had better at least ask if anyone had seen the outlaws, to which the answer was, 'Nobody ain't seen nothin', but the dog must've heard somebody durin' the night on account of he barked like hell'. Further questioning established that incident as being about one o'clock, which would probably be about right according to Caleb's reckoning.

Wally's prediction that they would find a dead horse before long suddenly came true as, on approaching a river, they did come across such a carcass, by that time swarming with flies and crows. It was difficult to see exactly where the horse had been injured, but a wound in the neck, now enlarged by the crows, appeared to be the obvious answer.

'Nothin' we can do about it now,' said Mick. 'Maybe we can collect the saddle later, if somebody don't beat us to it.' As they left the scene to cross the river, Caleb saw at least three foxes making their way towards an unexpected meal.

About a mile after crossing the river, Wally stopped and closely examined the ground, going on a few yards but returning to the original spot. After a time he pointed to his right.

'They went that way,' he said. 'They tried to cover their tracks but they didn't succeed very well.' He went on foot a few yards in the direction he had indicated and grunted with satisfaction. 'Yep!' he said. 'See that there ...' —he pointed at a clump of grass––'it's been trodden down. Yeh, they went this way all right.'

'Then it's plain that they don't know the

area,' said Mick Bywater. 'There's a ridge about two miles ahead and there ain't no way up, it must be more'n a hundred feet. That means that they either have to turn back north or follow the cliff south an' that leads to Warren Canyon. That's about twenty miles long and there definitely ain't no way out other than ride on through.'

'We could keep goin' and gain a lot of time,' suggested Wally.

'But we don't know which way they went when they reached the ridge,' Caleb pointed out. 'We can't assume that they continued south.'

'Guess not,' admitted Mick Bywater. 'OK, we keep followin' their tracks.'

'They must have rested up somewhere,' said Caleb. 'Their horses will need rest, if not them; and remember, one of them is now riding two up, which should slow them quite a bit, so be ready for them at any time.'

The first real sign that they were not too

far behind the outlaws came when they eventually reached the high cliffs of Warren Ridge, at the base of which flowed the quite narrow but turbulent River Warren. The sign came in the form of the still warm embers of a fire and indications of flattened grass where three people had obviously lain. A search of the area showed that the outlaws had turned back north and Caleb felt vindicated in insisting that they continue to follow the tracks. However, Wally appeared puzzled and continued to examine the area for some time.

'Somebody else is followin' 'em,' he eventually announced. 'That means that fire could've been the outlaws, or it could've been lit by whoever else is on their tail.'

'Are you quite sure?' asked Mick.

'Sure I'm sure,' grunted Wally. 'There's definitely been at least five, probably six, or maybe seven, horses through here recently and by recently I'd say within the last four hours at the outside.'

'So we know they headed north,' said Caleb, 'and we now know that there's somebody else following them. I think we can safely assume that that somebody else includes Aaron and Jed Jones and possibly two of their cronies. How far do these cliffs go?'

'About eight miles,' said Wally. 'Leastways, that's as far as they go before anyone could find a way up ridin' a horse.'

'And from there?' urged Caleb.

'Straight ahead, not goin' up, would bring them back to Bullhead, or pretty close to it,' said Mick. 'If they went up it's anybody's guess which direction they would go, although the trail is fairly well marked. It opens out on to a flat plain. Straight across brings you to a place called Pisa, not much of a place, a general store which is also a bar, maybe half a dozen houses, but nothin' else as far as I know. It's been a hell of a long time since I was there.'

'And I've only been through it once in my life,' added Wally, 'an' that was about thirty years ago. It didn't even have a store in those days.'

'How far?' asked Caleb.

Both men thought for a few moments before Mick eventually spoke. 'Maybe thirty miles,' he said. 'That's only a guess mind you, it could be less or it could be more.'

'And is the way up this ridge obvious?' asked Caleb.

'As plain as the nose on your face,' nodded Wally.

'Then I'd say that's the way they went,' said Caleb. 'OK, but from now on be on your guard for even more trouble.'

'The Jones brothers?' asked Mick.

'The Jones brothers,' confirmed Caleb.

The way up the ridge was indeed very obvious and was plainly used from time to time, a fact confirmed by Mick Bywater as it being on the main trail between

Bullhead and Pisa, although to the best of his knowledge very few people used it since there was no reason why anyone should want to go to Pisa or even Greenwood, a larger town some fifty miles beyond Pisa. However, Wally was quite adamant that there had been several horses that way quite recently, although he could not say exactly how many.

The road twisted and turned its way up the side of the ridge, now at least 150 feet high, and although it appeared wide enough to accommodate a wagon, there were several points where the road had collapsed and no attempt made to repair it. Once at the top, the terrain still twisted round large boulders and down and up hollows and would have provided anyone with almost perfect conditions to carry out an ambush. Caleb's eyes and ears were constantly on the alert.

By the time they reached the open plain, it was fast approaching nightfall and they eventually had to admit that there was little point in going on and made camp among a clump of trees alongside a small stream. Caleb and Mick Bywater cursed that neither of them had had the foresight to bring any food with them. However, Wally Barns came to the rescue and he returned to the camp after a short foray into the bush carrying a fairly large and most welcome rabbit.

He had warned them what he was doing and also warned them that they might hear a couple of shots. They had heard the shots and wondered if the sound had also reached the ears of whoever was in front of them. Wally also produced a bottle of coarse whiskey from his saddle-bag. He seemed quite happy to drink the rough liquid neat, but it proved too strong even for Caleb who claimed that he could drink most things, and he and Mick were forced to add water to their drink. Luckily Caleb had a tin mug, something he always carried, and he and Mick took turns sipping the whiskey and water while

Wally was quite content to take his straight from the bottle.

They had just settled down for the night when, in the distance, there came the distinct sound of gunfire. Immediately all three sat up and listened intently; there was more shooting for a short time and then it suddenly stopped.

'I'd say Sullivan has just had a run-in with the Jones brothers,' said Mick. 'I wonder who came off worst?'

'For my money I'd say the Jones brothers,' said Caleb. 'Frank Sullivan must've known they were being followed and they're far too experienced to allow amateurs like Jed and Aaron to get too close to them.'

'Probably,' conceded Mick. 'The thing is, they can't be too far ahead, do we wait until the morning or do we go after them now?'

'They should be easy enough to find,' said Wally.

'If they're still alive,' said Caleb. 'The

decision is yours, Deputy,' he added.

Mick thought for a few moments. 'We go now,' he decided. 'I can't see Sullivan stayin' there until the mornin' and we can't afford to lose them now. We'll just have to take a chance on meetin' up with Jed an' Aaron or findin' their bodies.'

Their horses were quickly saddled and they set off in the direction of the shooting, although they were forced to travel slowly due to the unknown terrain and because there was very little moonlight.

By Caleb's estimation, they must have been travelling about an hour, during which time they had covered no more than about six miles, when Wally suddenly hissed the command to stop.

'There's a fire over there,' he whispered. Both Caleb and Mick peered into the darkness but could see nothing. 'Believe me, there is,' said Wally. 'I might have gone a bit rusty on some things, but there's nothin' wrong with my eyes. It's about a hundred yards over there.' Once again both Caleb and Mick peered into the gloom but had to admit defeat, but they were quite prepared to accept what Wally said. 'The best thing is to walk,' continued Wally. 'We can lead the horses until we're almost on top of them.' Caleb and Mick agreed that this was probably the best plan and all three dismounted, Wally taking the lead.

It was about ten minutes later when Wally nudged Caleb and pointed, but by that time Caleb had also seen the glow of the fire. They tethered their horses to a bush and, with Wally once again leading, they slowly made their way towards the glow.

They stopped about twenty yards from the fire and could see three shadowy figures huddled round the flames and from the reflection of the flames on two of their faces, it was obvious that it was Jed and Aaron Jones and one other. This time it was Caleb who took charge of the situation and motioned Wally to go round to the right and Mick to go round to the left.

'Don't shoot unless you have to,' Caleb instructed. 'Leave the talking to me.'

Both men did as instructed and Caleb gave them a couple of minutes to get into position before he boldly—but somewhat foolishly he thought later walked towards the fire. Immediately there was something of a panic amongst them, but no attempt to shoot, which was rather surprising, Caleb thought.

'Who the hell's there?' demanded one of them. Caleb remained silent but continued towards them. Eventually they recognized him and even seemed somewhat relieved. 'Mr Black!' said Jed Jones. 'What the hell are you doin' out here?'

'The same as you, it would appear,' replied Caleb. 'Chasing outlaws.' He called out to Mick and Wally. 'It's OK, they don't seem to have any guns.' Mick and Wally appeared out of the darkness, each ready with their guns just in case.

'Mick!' sighed Jed 'And ain't that Wally Barns?'

'Right first time,' said Mick. 'We heard shootin'; what's been goin' on?'

'They surprised us,' said Aaron. 'Just came at us out of the dark, just like you. They killed Tom Wiesensky; that's his body over there ...' He indicated something lying on the ground a few yards away.

'An' I took a bullet in my arm,' said the other youth with them.

'Des Coltrane,' said Mick. 'I might've guessed you an' Tom would be involved. Are you hurt bad?'

'Went straight through,' said Des. 'I still need to see Doc Campbell pretty quick though.'

'You're a long way from Bullhead,' said Caleb. 'So what happened?'

'The bastards took our horses,' muttered Jed. 'We was lucky they didn't kill us all, but they only seemed interested in the horses.'

'You must've seen the dead one,' said

184

Wally. 'Don't you have any horses?'

'Took 'em all, as far as we know,' said Jed. 'We ain't really looked though, we can't see nothin' in the dark.'

'And it was probably the dark which saved you,' said Caleb. 'OK, I guess there's not a lot we can do about it tonight. We'll stay here and look for them in the morning.'

'There's just one question I'd like an answer to,' said Mick. 'How the hell did they get hold of them guns? They must've had outside help and my money is on you pair; I can't see anyone else doin' it.'

'That'd be against the law,' objected Jed 'We wouldn't do nothin' that was against the law.'

'Pardon me if I don't believe you,' said Mick. 'All I can say is that you have a lot of questions to answer once you're back at Bullhead an' Mr McCready knows how to get the truth out of anyone.'

'And I believe it will mean a long time

in prison for helping outlaws to escape,' said Caleb.

'I didn't have nothin' to do with it!' objected Des Coltrane. 'I told 'em it was a crazy idea.'

'You'll be able to explain all that to Mr McCready,' said Mick. 'It looks like you have a problem about gettin' back to Bullhead though. With no horses it seems that you have a long walk in front of you.'

'What about Tom?' moaned Aaron. 'You can't leave him here.'

'Why not?' said Caleb. 'He isn't going anywhere and he certainly can't walk with you. You could try carrying him I suppose.'

'You have to take us all back to Bullhead,' insisted Aaron. 'You have to, it's your duty.'

'Our first duty is to get them outlaws back in jail,' said Mick. 'Maybe if you wait here we just might call back an' take you with us.'

'You might not come back,' objected Des Coltrane. 'You might get killed.'

'That's a chance you'll just have to take,' laughed Caleb.

'But we can't just leave Tom's body out here,' moaned Jed 'The buzzards an' wolves will eat him.'

'Then he'll've served some useful purpose in life,' said Mick. 'You'll have to bury him. He can always be dug up later if that's what his family wants, although I don't think his pa will be all that bothered, they ain't seen eye-to-eye for years. His ma died a couple of years ago an' his pa's new wife hates his guts.'

'You're just goin' to leave us here?' grunted Jed. 'That figures. We ain't nobody. We ain't important enough for anyone to want to worry about.'

'That just about says it all,' agreed Mick.

187

EIGHT

Although the youths had not attempted to use any guns against Caleb the previous night, they had in fact been armed, Jed having an Adams pistol and an ancient Nutting revolving chamber rifle, Aaron, an even older magazine-loading Buchel rifle, Des Coltrane, a more modern Colt pistol and Tom Wiesensky, a shotgun. Caleb had expected the Jones brothers to try to steal their horses during the night and had positioned himself between them and the animals, but in the event his fears had proved groundless and the only effect of his vigil was to deprive him of his sleep, although he was well used to going the odd night without any. They were up and ready to leave just before dawn, the three youths complaining that they were hungry and had not eaten for about twenty-four hours, but they received scant sympathy from the others and were told do some hunting.

Despite pleas and protests, Caleb, Wally and the deputy rode out just as first light was showing over the hills, Caleb suggesting that the best thing the youths could do was bury Tom Wiesensky and then start walking back to Bullhead.

Finding the tracks of the outlaws proved very easy. Even Caleb found little difficulty in reading the signs. After about two hours they came across further indications that they had spent the night camped in a hollow, but this time there had been no fire so there was no indication of just how far ahead they were, although it was agreed that it could not possibly be more than two hours, on the assumption that they, too, had continued at dawn.

Up to that point there had been no sign of any of the horses and since it was known that they had taken the four horses belonging to the youths and had two of their own, Caleb would have expected them to abandon the three they did not need somewhere along the way. It was another two hours before they came upon the abandoned horses, each still saddled, amongst a clump of trees alongside a river The animals appeared contented enough and it was agreed that the best thing that could be done for them was to unsaddle them and leave them free to roam on the assumption that they would not stray too far from either good grazing or water. The saddles were hidden amongst some bushes to be recovered at some future time.

From that point onwards, according to Wally Barns, the pace of the outlaws quickened, although signs of their progress were still easy to follow. There were a couple of places where it appeared trails crossed and Wally took some time to establish exactly which way they had gone, which on both occasions was straight ahead towards Pisa. At midday, they came to the junction of two rivers, where the trail divided, one forking off to the right alongside the now widened river and the other fork crossing both rivers. A sign indicated that the road to Pisa was through the fords, although Caleb was of the opinion that the right fork was the better used. However, all agreed that it would be foolish to ignore the signpost.

Once through the fords, Wally Barns searched for clues and appeared satisfied that the outlaws had also chosen that way, pointing out the still damp tracks, although the presence of a small herd of deer not far away cast some doubt on this assertion in Caleb's mind, but then he reminded himself that he could never tell one set of animal prints from another. Even if they were on the right road, the signpost had given no indication as to just how far ahead Pisa lay. Mick Bywater was of the opinion that it could not be more than ten miles.

Mick's estimate proved to be very

accurate and less than an hour later the three were standing amongst some trees looking down on what was, apparently, the town of Pisa. As Mick had said, it was hardly large enough to be called a town, but the sign a few yards further down the road insisted that it was.

In a hollow alongside a narrow river, there were eight buildings, two paddocks and an assortment of cultivated strips of land. Apart from two dogs roaming the street, Pisa appeared deserted, but that could have been easily explained by the habit of most country folk of having a siesta in the afternoon. The hillsides around the town, on both sides of the river, were covered in trees and the only road snaked away from the town to be quickly lost in the forest. It appeared that both Mick Bywater and Wally Barns were waiting for Caleb to decide what to do. Caleb smiled and nodded, realizing that Mick did not have the experience and Wally simply did not want to become any more involved than he already was.

'I reckon they're down there,' said Caleb, 'and I don't think they've been here very long. See those three horses in that paddock? They're still saddled and two of them don't look like working animals. Folk like these don't normally waste money on animals they can't work. Those three horses we found were working horses and one of them down there is probably more used to pulling a wagon than being ridden. The other two are definitely riding horses though.'

'That kind of reasonin' would never've occurred to me,' admitted Wally. 'To me a horse is a horse, but I see what you mean.'

'Mr Black,' said Mick, 'I know it's me who has the badge, but I must admit that I am completely out of my depth. I hope you'll understand if I hand things over to you. I hear that you were an officer in the army, so you must be used to making decisions and, as a minister, you must be used to folk lookin' to you.'

Caleb grinned and nodded. 'Sure, I don't mind, but you just remember to do exactly what I tell you. Now, on the assumption that Sullivan is down there, probably in the bar, whichever shack that is ...'

'The big one in the centre, I think,' pointed Mick.

'Probably,' agreed Caleb. 'OK, since they don't appear to be about, we must assume that's where they are. Now, I have been thinking and all sorts of ideas have passed through my mind on the way here, but now I see the place the choices are very limited. It would be very foolish for the three of us to simply ride into the town; we'd probably be dead before we reached the bar ...'

'Not me,' said Wally, very firmly. 'My job was to track them outlaws an' that's just what I done. Nobody said nothin' about any shootin'. I got me a family back in Bullhead to consider. You do whatever you have to, but count me out.'

'You can't back out now, Wally ...' said Mick.

'I ain't backin' out,' said Wally. 'All I said was I done my bit in gettin' you this far. That's all I was asked to do an' that's all I intend to do. I ain't no lawman nor no bounty hunter.'

'That's OK, Wally,' said Caleb. 'You've done exactly what was asked of you. From now on it's up to Mick and me, although why I should bother I'm not sure; I did my bit in arresting them in the first place. However, it seems that I am committed to more. You stay here, Wally, you should be safe enough. Deputy, I want you to circle round behind the town and come in behind the bar. I'll take it from the front.'

'But you said they'd kill you as soon as they see you,' said Mick.

Caleb laughed. 'In that case you'll be on your own,' he said. 'I don't think that'll happen though, not if I'm on my own.

195

If there'd been you or Wally, then they probably would've shot first. If I go in on my own, a man like Sullivan will be curious. He'll want to know how I found him; he'll want to gloat over my death and a bullet too early would deprive him of his pleasure. I don't suppose Pisa has anything like a sheriff?'

'It never used to have one,' said Mick. 'As far as I know it's covered by the sheriff of Marigold County and he works out of Greenwood.'

'And Greenwood is about fifty miles away,' nodded Caleb. 'That's a big area to cover. The chances are that they hardly ever see a lawman.'

'If it's anythin' like Bullhead used to be about twenty years ago,' said Wally, 'They don't need one. It's the type of place hardly anyone has a need to go to an' they're such a close-knit community they deal with all their own problems.'

'I've been there many times,' grinned Caleb. 'OK, Deputy, I'll give you time to get into position. Just make sure nobody sees you. It looks like cutting along the side of that hill is about the best way if you keep to the line of trees. You just make sure that you're on hand should I need you.'

'Yes sir, Mr Black, sir,' said Mick. 'You can rely on me.'

The deputy went on foot and was soon lost amongst the trees and it seemed an eternity before Caleb saw him step briefly into the open, above the town, obviously indicating that he was ready. On seeing him, Caleb mounted his horse and rode slowly down the hill, leaving Wally with instructions that should anything go wrong, he was not to place himself in danger but was to return to Bullhead as fast as he could.

The two dogs which Caleb had seen earlier came rushing forward, barking and snarling and for a moment he was tempted to shoot both of them, but suddenly an elderly man appeared from the first shack and shouted at the dogs, both of which very reluctantly backed off, snarling and baring their teeth. The man looked strangely at Caleb and grabbed at both animals.

'That makes four of you,' he drawled. 'We ain't seen one for years an' suddenly there's four. Your friends are in the bar an' I'll give you the same advice I gave them, do your business an' get on your way, we don't like strangers in Pisa.'

'Especially black strangers,' smiled Caleb. The man did not reply. 'In the bar you say,' he continued. 'Where's that?'

'Big buildin' over there,' grunted the man. 'The one with the pots an' pans hangin' on the wall.' Caleb raised his hat slightly, smiled and rode on.

He was quite certain that by that time his arrival had been seen by the outlaws and he was braced for action, although he did not really expect any at that moment. As he rode up to the building, Frank Sullivan appeared in the doorway, his thumbs hooked in the top of his jeans, a gun protruding from his waist-band. For a few moments both men stared mockingly at each other.

'Afternoon, Reveren',' Sullivan smiled sardonically. 'I was sorta expectin' you. I'm surprised you is alone though.'

'The sheriff hadn't come back,' said Caleb, as he dismounted and tethered his horse. 'The deputy couldn't leave town so I came on my own. Leastways, I thought I was on my own but I came across the Jones brothers and two of their cronies—well, one of their cronies, the other one was dead, killed by one of you so they said.'

'Could be,' agreed Sullivan, 'we never stopped to find out. What you come after us for, Reveren'?'

'No bodies, no money,' said Caleb. 'I'm not in the habit of losing bodies or letting that much money slip through my hands.'

'And you think you can take us back?' laughed Sullivan. 'We don't make the same mistake twice. We could gun you down right here an' now,'

'You could try,' invited Caleb, flicking aside the tails of his coat to reveal his two guns. 'I don't wear two just for show.' Sullivan licked his lips and looked towards the door as if looking for guidance or assistance but none appeared to be coming his way. Neither Winston nor Grant showed themselves. 'Your move,' said Caleb.

'Reveren',' said Frank, easing himself away from the wall. 'We kinda like you, we don't wanna kill you. Sorry about the money, but as far as we're concerned our freedom is worth a whole lot more'n a few dollars. Let's just say you put this one down to experience an' we can all ride out of here. If you don't, it's more'n like you'll end up dead an', like I said, we don't really want to kill you.'

'I can't say that I feel the same about you,' said Caleb. 'It'd sure save me a whole lot of trouble if I took you back dead.'

'But you won't,' said Frank. 'You need us to tell the judge that them Jones boys must've murdered their own ma an' pa before we arrived an' then murdered their own sisters after we'd left.'

'It really doesn't matter to me what happens to them,' said Caleb. 'There's nothing in it for me.'

'Except maybe a bullet,' sneered Winston Marshall, making a brief appearance in the doorway but then disappearing just as quickly.

Caleb was very curious; he would have expected at least one of them to have attempted to do something by that time and there was something about the demeanour of Frank Sullivan which told him that they were not about to. As he remembered it, their guns were five-shot Adams and, remembering that they had left Bullhead armed only with these and had not had the opportunity to acquire more bullets, he assumed that they had been limited to fifteen shots in total. They had obviously wasted some of their precious ammunition in the shootout between themselves and the youths, perhaps even having used all their bullets. He decided to take a gamble.

Immediately Caleb drew his guns, Frank Sullivan ducked back into the store, slamming the door behind him, but there were no retaliatory shots. After a short time there came a shout from Sullivan that they were coming out, but also warning Caleb that they had a hostage. The hostage, in the form of an elderly woman, appeared in the doorway with Grant Marshall holding a knife to her throat.

'I was right,' said Caleb. 'You haven't got any ammunition and a place like this is most unlikely to have any.'

'OK, Mr Smart Ass,' said Grant, 'but we do have this woman an' we do have her old man as well. Now I'll tell you exactly what you're goin' to do. Our horses are in the paddock saddled and ready to go ...'

'We take his horse,' came the voice of

Winston Marshall. 'That old nag I'm ridin' ain't fit for nothin' but haulin' a wagon. We take his horse, that way he'll never be able to catch us.'

'Hear that?' sneered Grant. 'You go bring our two horses round here. After that we take the woman with us until we're sure you ain't followin' an' then we'll let her go.'

'And if I don't?' replied Caleb.

'Then I slit her throat an' her old man gets the same treatment,' said Grant.

'And then you all end up dead,' smiled Caleb.

'And you'll have the death of these people on your conscience,' called Winston.

'I don't have any conscience,' laughed Caleb. 'These people mean nothing to me. At this moment five thousand five hundred dollars is all that matters.'

'Don't play games with us!' shouted Frank Sullivan. 'You do just as Grant says.'

'I don't play games,' said Caleb. 'OK,

go ahead, slit her throat, see how far it gets you.'

'Damn you!' cried the woman. 'They tell me you're a preacher. If that's true, you can't just stand by while they murder us. Do like they say—please!'

Caleb had little doubt that the threat to the woman and her husband would be carried out and, despite his talk, he knew that he simply could not let that happen. He slowly holstered his guns and nodded.

'OK,' he conceded, 'but there's just one thing: the woman and her husband stay here. You can ride out and I won't try to shoot you, but she stays here.'

'She stays here provided you hand over your guns,' said Frank. 'Your two guns and your rifle plus all the ammunition you have.'

'First I get your horses,' said Caleb. 'That way I can be sure you won't shoot me in the back.'

'OK,' agreed Frank. 'You go get the

horses, but leave yours here.'

Caleb patted his horse and made his way round the back of the building to the paddock and managed to grab hold of the two animals concerned. Suddenly there was a hiss to his right which he knew came from the deputy. He did not look just in case one of the outlaws was watching.

'Just like I thought,' he whispered in response. 'They've used up all their ammunition and there's no more to be had and apparently no guns either.'

'What's happenin' now then?' hissed Mick, apparently from behind a small stack of hay.

'They've got hostages,' said Caleb. 'I have to take these two horses round to them. They're taking mine as well. You make sure you're in a position to shoot as soon as they start to ride out, but with a bit of luck there'll only be one of them.'

'What you mean?' whispered Mick.

'What I say,' hissed Caleb. 'Now, you

just be ready an' stop asking questions.'

He led the animals out of the paddock, closing the gate behind him, which meant that his back was facing the rear of the store-cum-bar. His hand moved deftly under the one animal and he continued to lead them round to the front. There was one brief moment when he was behind a small shed and out of sight of any possible watchers, during which time his hand slipped under the other horse. As he led them back into view, he noticed a black face peering at him through a small window. He pretended that he had not seen him.

At the front of the building he was greeted by Grant Marshall still holding the woman and Winston Marshall also with a knife held to an old man's throat. Frank Sullivan stood with his thumbs tucked into the tops of his jeans, smiling sardonically.

'Now, your guns,' he said. 'Real slow now, no sudden movements or the woman

gets it first. Just the guns, not the belts.'
Caleb slowly drew both his Colts and
handed them to Sullivan, who weighed
both in his hands and then tossed one to
Grant. 'The rifle can stay where it is,' he
continued. 'What about bullets?'

'Apart from the few in my belts,' said
Caleb, 'There's two boxes of thirty for the
Colts and one box of twenty for the rifle
in my saddle-bags.'

'Them bullets in your belt,' said Frank.
'Hand 'em over.' Caleb did as instructed,
handing them to Frank who pushed them
into his pocket.

'You done well, Reveren',' sneered
Winston. 'It's almost a pity to have to
kill you.'

'Leave him!' ordered Frank. 'I kinda like
the guy an' besides, it could be bad luck to
murder a priest. You can let the man an'
woman go now, there ain't nobody goin'
to do nothin' an' we got us some decent
guns.'

'I thought you said we was goin' to kill

him,' objected Winston. 'I was lookin' forward to it.'

'I said leave him!' snarled Frank again. 'Get mounted an' let's get out of here. He'll never be able to keep up with us on that old horse in the paddock.' Frank raised his hat slightly in salute to Caleb. 'Us black folk have to stick together, Reveren',' he continued. 'That's the one thing what saved you this time, the colour of your skin. I ain't never killed no black brother yet, especially no preacher. Don't come lookin' for us, Reveren', the next time I might just forget that you is black an' a preacherman.'

Winston pushed the old man to one side and mounted Caleb's horse and was followed by Frank Sullivan, Grant waited until the other two were mounted before climbing on to his horse. For a moment all three stared down at Caleb and sneered.

'Let's go!' ordered Frank.

They swung the horses round and dug their heels into the horses' flanks. The animals responded immediately, Winston, on Caleb's horse, leading the way. Caleb held his breath for a few seconds and then smiled with satisfaction as Grant Marshall's saddle suddenly slipped off his horse, throwing him on to the ground. Frank Sullivan swerved to avoid Grant and immediately found himself also crashing to the ground, his saddle landing on top of him, obviously causing some pain. Winston apparently had not realized what was happening until a shout from Caleb alerted Deputy Mick Bywater.

It was impossible to tell which happened first, but Caleb leapt forward, grabbed the gun out of Grant's jeans and barked at Frank Sullivan to stay where he was. There was a single shot which sent Winston Marshall reeling from his horse. Deputy Bywater was very quickly standing over Winston, his gun aimed unerringly at his chest.

'Well done, Deputy,' grinned Caleb. 'That was close.'

'What the hell happened?' asked Mick.

'Just a little trick I've used before,' smiled Caleb. 'OK, Sullivan, you're not hurt that bad, on your feet; you, too, Marshall.' Both the Marshalls struggled to their feet. Despite Caleb's assurance that Frank Sullivan was not too badly hurt, it was plain that he was in a great deal of pain as he clutched at his shoulder. Winston, too, was plainly injured, blood now staining his shirt as he too clutched at his upper arm. All three were herded back to the store-cum-bar where Caleb cursorily examined both men and found that Frank Sullivan had suffered a broken collar bone and Winston nothing more than a bullet lodged in his upper arm.

'You'll both live,' he declared.

'I told you we should've killed the bastard!' grated Winston.

'I'll listen to you next time,' grunted Frank. 'That was very clever of you, Reveren',' he said to Caleb. 'I was watchin' you all the time but I never saw you do anythin'. I reckon you must've somehow cut them straps.'

'Just enough not to be obvious,' smiled Caleb. 'Sometimes it works pretty good, like it did just now, but sometimes it doesn't happen quite so soon. I guess I was lucky and you were unlucky. That's one reason I always keep a sharp knife handy.'

'So that's how it was done,' nodded Mick Bywater. 'I must admit, I was watching you too and I never saw nothin'.'

'That's because neither of you were expecting anything like that,' said Caleb. 'Now, we have two useless saddles. I guess that means that two of you will have to ride bareback. You have the worst injury, Sullivan, you can ride the horse with the saddle.'

By that time Wally Barns, who had been witness to everything from the safety of the hill, had ridden into Pisa leading Mick Bywater's horse and he was sent to bring the remaining horse from the paddock. In the meantime, Caleb had checked that the woman and the man were not injured and, possibly to quell his feelings of guilt, he purchased two bottles of rough whiskey.

'Sorry if I seemed as though I couldn't care less,' he apologized to them both, 'but those three are very dangerous men. Still, everything's all right now; at least I hope it is.'

'All I can say is it was a good job the deputy was on hand,' grumbled the old man. 'Where you from, son, I ain't seen you around before?'

'Bullhead,' said Mick. 'Sheriff Mc-Cready's deputy. These men had escaped from our jail.'

'McCready,' nodded the man. 'Sure, I know him. I ain't seen him for a few years though, didn't even know if he was still alive.' He looked at Caleb. 'You sure dress like a preacher,' he said to him. 'First time I ever seen a preacher wearin' a gun though.'

'I am fully ordained,' smiled Caleb.

'Ain't never seen a black preacher before,' said the woman, 'but then we ain't seen no kind of preacher in Pisa for about two years. There's one or two here who could do with someone like you.'

Caleb smiled. 'I don't have any plans, I could come back after I've settled things at Bullhead.' The man and woman looked at each other for a moment. 'If you don't want me here, I understand,' continued Caleb, 'not everyone appreciates someone like me.'

'There's three christenin's an' two weddin's that need attendin' to,' said the woman. 'Don't you worry none about what other folk here think, they'll do as they're told; I'm grandmother to most of 'em.'

'I'll be back then,' Caleb said.

NINE

Pisa did not have anything like a secure place in which to keep the outlaws and nowhere other than on the floor of one of the small sheds, or the floor of the bar where Wally, Mick Bywater and Caleb could sleep, but after inspecting the shed, all three decided that they would rather sleep in a nearby pigsty. In the end it was agreed that all six would have to spend the night on the floor of the store-cum-bar. Even though they were in the same room, Caleb was taking no chances and tied the outlaws securely. The only concession he made was to Frank Sullivan's broken collar bone, leaving his left arm free, safe in the knowledge that it would be far too painful for Sullivan to move his arm much. Apart from a few threats early on from

Winston and Grant Marshall, the night passed peacefully enough.

Breakfast, for those who wanted any, consisted of dry bread and porridge. Caleb refused, although he did take a large chunk of greyish bread just in case he felt hungry later. Their departure was witnessed by what must have been the entire population of Pisa, perhaps fifty people in all, including children. The previous evening those same people had gathered round when it had become plain that the outlaws were no longer any threat. Various wayward children had been brought into line by not-so-subtle hints that they would be fed to the outlaws since it was a known fact that all black men were cannibals. It seemed that the adults were inclined to believe this even if the children tended not to.

Frank Sullivan was helped on to the only other horse with a saddle while Winston and Grant Marshall were forced to ride bareback. Caleb once again tied a length of rope to one ankle of each man, passed it under the horse and then firmly tied it to the other ankle, warning both Winston and Grant to make sure that they did not fall off. Grant protested that he had never ridden a saddleless horse before to which Caleb sneeringly replied that he was about to learn something new.

Half an hour after sunrise, they rode out of Pisa, Caleb deliberately taking a slow pace to allow the two bareback riders to become accustomed to their horses. It was almost midday when they came upon the site where they had left the other horses, which were still contentedly grazing.

The saddles were brought from the bushes where they had been hidden, but it was obvious that they were too big to put on Winston's and Grant's horses, so the pair were transferred to two of the larger, working horses.

By five o'clock they had reached the spot where they had last seen the Jones brothers. There was no sign of them and

Caleb would have been very surprised had they still been there. Neither had there been any attempt to bury Tom Wiesnesky and the crows and foxes had been feasting, his partly eaten and now rather smelly body exactly where it had been before. Grant Marshall, as the only completely fit outlaw, was given the task of digging a hole. Caleb, in his capacity of preacher, conducted a brief service over the grave. Wally Barns set out to look for some game and returned half an hour later with a young deer.

'Any sign of them?' asked Caleb, referring to the Jones brothers and Des Coltrane.

'Not that I could see,' replied Wally, 'but I didn't look along the trail, I'll go take a look if you want me to.'

'No need,' nodded Caleb. 'We'll pick them up easily enough tomorrow.'

Wally did pick up the trail left by the youths quite easily, but it appeared that they had made better headway than might have been expected and by mid-afternoon they had still not overtaken them.

By that time they were among the rocks and hollows at the top of Warren Ridge and Caleb felt very uneasy. They were now in perfect ambush country and he was quite certain that the Jones brothers were still determined to kill Frank Sullivan and the Marshalls if they could. He drew his rifle and rode with it at the ready.

'Expectin' trouble?' asked Frank Sullivan.

'Could be,' nodded Caleb. 'There's three young men who were screaming for your blood up in those rocks somewhere.'

'Then maybe you'd better give us some guns,' grinned Sullivan. 'We got a right to defend ourselves.'

'The only rights you have are what either me or the deputy give you,' said Caleb. 'You just keep your eyes open and yell if you see anything.'

'Do you really think they would be

stupid enough to ambush us?' asked Mick Bywater. 'That'd put them outside the law too.'

'They're young enough and stupid enough to try anything,' replied Caleb. 'The one thing they don't want is these three standing up in court and claiming that the brothers murdered their own family. It might be very difficult to prove anything against them, but there would always be that suspicion and I don't think the farmers as a whole would want possible murderers living among them.'

They had travelled about two miles since entering the rock-strewn slopes of Warren Ridge when they came upon a section of the trail which passed through a narrow gully for a distance of what appeared to be about 200 yards, sheer rocks on either side and very few places in which to take cover. Caleb called a halt before they entered the gully and sent Wally to the left whilst he went to the right partly to see if there was any way round and partly to see if there was any sign of the youths. Both returned ten minutes later shaking their heads.

'Only way is straight through,' said Wally. 'As for the Jones boys, they could be almost anywhere. Climbin' the sides would be easy enough, but there ain't no way a horse could get up.'

'Same this side,' nodded Caleb. 'Maybe I'm just being over-cautious and suspicious, but I'd rather be safe than sorry. Are you ready to risk going through?' Wally and Mick Bywater looked at each other and nodded, each checking that their guns were loaded.

'Don't we have no say in the matter?' demanded Frank Sullivan. 'We is the ones who'll get shot first.'

'You have no say in anything,' Caleb laughed. 'There is just one thing I will do for you though; perhaps I should have done it before. I will untie your ankles just in case you have to jump off.' He nodded to Wally and Mick who each untied one of them and Caleb untied Frank Sullivan.

'All right,' he said eventually. 'Let's start moving. Wally, you keep your eye on anything up to the left, Deputy, you concentrate on what lies ahead and I'll watch for anything on the right.'

They started forward, moving very slowly. Caleb would have liked to have travelled much faster, but neither space nor the type of horses the outlaws were riding would allow that. They had moved about half the distance along the gully and Caleb was beginning to think that perhaps he had been over-cautious, when a sudden movement a few yards ahead and up to his right made him shout and warn the others. Immediately, there was a shot, quickly followed by more and Frank Sullivan fell to the ground with blood streaming from his head. Winston and Grant leapt off their horses, closely followed by Wally Barns.

'Go!' ordered Caleb, slapping the rear end of the deputy's horse.

The combination of shooting and the sudden slap on its rear end terrified the animal and Mick Bywater was unable to do little else except hang on. A couple of shots followed him but they quickly returned to those in the gully, the main targets definitely Frank Sullivan and the Marshalls. Caleb, too, leapt off his horse and found some protection in a narrow crevice. It appeared that someone was on either side of the gully.

The shooting continued with Frank Sullivan lying in the middle of the track, apparently dead, although Caleb did detect a twitch of the mouth. Grant Marshall yelled in pain as a bullet tore into his arm just below his elbow and Wally Barns grunted as he too took a bullet in his leg.

'You'll never get away with this!' called Caleb.

'With all of you dead, who the hell's to say what happened?' came the reply.

'Mick Bywater has got through,' reminded Caleb.

'That's what you think,' laughed the

voice. 'Right now he's lyin' in a pool of blood. He looks very dead.' Caleb cursed himself for sending the deputy through and also cursed himself for being so stupid as to knowingly fall into such a trap. 'We can soon arrange things to make it look like you all had a shoot-out an' killed each other,' continued the voice, which Caleb assumed belonged to Jed Jones

'You don't think anyone would believe you, do you?'

'It don't matter what anyone thinks,' said another voice, this time from the other side of the gully. 'Nobody would have no proof of anythin' an' that's all that matters.'

'Just like nobody would be able to prove that you murdered your own parents and sisters if Sullivan and the Marshalls were dead,' called Caleb.

'Somethin' like that,' said the voice, this time plainly that of Aaron Jones 'Anyhow, Pa had it comin'; he was about to disown us. Jed lost his temper and slit his throat.

Ma saw him do it so he had to kill her as well.'

'What about your sisters?' urged Caleb, anxious to keep them talking while he looked for a way up the rocks.

'That was me,' said Aaron, almost proudly. 'They was allus teasin' me, sayin' as how I was no good an' how all the girls in the valley an' in Bullhead laughed at me. They both found out I can't be messed with.'

'Very interesting!' boomed another voice from somewhere above the brothers. 'Drop those guns, Jed, Aaron an' whoever that is with you.'

'McCready!' called Caleb. 'What kept you?'

'Sheriff McCready?' cried Aaron. 'Hear that, Jed, he's up there. We don't stand a chance. Let's get the hell out of here.'

'I've had enough,' called Des Coltrane. 'I didn't have nothin' to do with murderin' their ma an' pa. Don't shoot, Sheriff, I'm comin' out without my gun.'

'Jed?' called Aaron.

Jed and Aaron had been on the same side of the gully, opposite to where Sheriff McCready now stood. When there was no reply from his brother, Aaron clambered up the rocks, managing to dodge shots from both Caleb and Sheriff McCready. By that time, Des Coltrane had appeared on the trail, unarmed and his hands high in the air.

'Mick is lying on the track,' called Sheriff McCready. 'Mr Black, you keep an eye on things down there, I'm goin' to see if there's anythin' I can do for him.'

Caleb's first task was to examine Wally Barns. He found that the bullet was still lodged in his leg, but the injury was not life-threatening. Frank Sullivan, too, was still alive; the bullet had simply made a deep graze in the side of his head. It looked a lot worse than it actually was, although he was still unconscious. Grant Marshall's wound was little more than a minor discomfort, the bullet having passed straight through. The horses were still very uneasy and it took Caleb quite a long time to quieten them down. Even Des Coltrane, anxious to show that he was simply an innocent party, did his bit in soothing the animals. Fifteen minutes later, Sheriff McCready appeared.

'He'll be all right,' said the sheriff as he approached, referring to his deputy. 'He'll have a bit of a headache for a while, but there doesn't appear to be any serious damage.'

'Same with Sullivan,' said Caleb. 'You arrived just in time, Sheriff. I don't think I've ever been so pleased to see the law before. What made you come out this way?'

'I got back into Bullhead the day after you left. I had to make a detour round a landslide on the way back,' said McCready. 'By that time it was too late to even think about startin' out after you. I picked up your trail easy enough though, except that I could've saved a whole lot of time if I'd come direct.'

'How did you know they were waitin' for us?' asked Wally.

'They weren't expectin' anyone from that direction,' laughed McCready. 'I saw them an' waited, but I couldn't get any closer. It was obvious that they were plannin' an' ambush. I couldn't get into position until they started shooting. Anyhow, it's p'raps as well I did wait, I heard everythin' they said an' that's more'n enough to convict them.'

'But they've got away,' said Wally.

'I'll worry about them later,' he replied. 'Right now the important thing is to get the injured back to Bullhead.'

It took them another three hours to reach Bullhead and they had not seen anyone on the way but, as ever, the bush telegraph system was well ahead of them and they were greeted by a large crowd.

227

By that time, Mick Bywater had recovered consciousness although he was still plainly very groggy. Sheriff McCready insisted that the doctor attend his deputy before anyone else. Next came Wally Barns and the outlaws last of all.

Des Coltrane was locked in the jail along with Winston and Grant Marshall, all in separate cells. Frank Sullivan was treated in the doctor's house since he was still unconscious. It also gave the doctor the chance to straighten out the broken collar bone as much as he could without having his patient cry and writhe in pain. When he eventually did come round, he, too, was placed in the jail.

The mayor busied round full of self-importance and only succeeded in annoying Sheriff McCready. Caleb had taken the opportunity to get out of the way and went to sleep for the remainder of the day. Deputy Bywater, too, was told to rest.

When Caleb did finally emerge, Mayor Sanderson appeared to have quietened down and the initial excitement which had spread throughout the town had almost disappeared. Caleb went along to the saloon and was told that Sheriff McCready wanted to see him. He drank a small glass of beer and then wandered off to the sheriff's office.

'You wanted to see me, Mr McCready?' he said as he went in.

'Just had this telegram,' answered the sheriff, waving a piece of paper. 'There's a US Marshal and two deputies due in in the mornin'. They'll be on the mornin' train into Kingston—that's the nearest the railroad comes, about ten miles due east. Anyhow, this Marshal ...' —he looked at the telegram—'Bill Crabtree, knows Frank Sullivan, so if he identifies him, you can collect your money. They should be here by nine o'clock.'

'I think I've earned it,' smiled Caleb. 'I don't normally have to catch outlaws twice. How's Mick?'

'Apart from a sore head, he's fine,'

replied the sheriff. 'He says he'll be back workin' in the mornin'.'

'What about the Jones brothers?' asked Caleb.

Sheriff McCready's answer was interrupted by Mayor Sanderson bursting into the office. He looked at Caleb and smiled sardonically. 'It's been agreed,' he said, addressing the sheriff. 'Five hundred dollars each.' He looked at Caleb again and sneered slightly. 'Alive!'

'I take it you are talking about Jed and Aaron Jones,' said Caleb.

'Of course,' said the mayor. 'We think five hundred dollars each is a fair reward. I suppose it is too small to interest you, particularly as you are about to come into more than five thousand.'

'I've hunted men for less,' smiled Caleb. 'The least I ever picked up was twenty-five dollars for some local layabout I happened to come across. I've regularly had to settle for fifty dollars.'

'Personally, I would be much happier

if you weren't interested,' said the mayor. 'We seem to have had more trouble in the short time you have been in Bullhead than we've had for the last twenty years.'

'Then I won't bother,' Caleb shrugged. 'I can take a hint.'

'Good,' sniffed the mayor. 'I suppose Mr McCready has told you that the authorities will be here tomorrow?' Caleb nodded. 'I have alerted the bank to the likelihood of having to pay you, so there should be no problems and nothing to detain you. I think we can deal with the Joneses in our own way.'

'Which is why you are offering a reward of five hundred dollars apiece!' grinned Caleb. 'I wish more towns dealt with their problems like that, I'd be a rich man.'

'They won't get far!' humphed the mayor. 'They don't have any horses, remember.'

'Which means they'll kill to get them,' said Caleb.

The three lawmen rode into Bullhead as predicted, at exactly nine o'clock. Bill Crabtree took one look at Frank Sullivan and pronounced himself satisfied. He did not say anything when he saw Caleb and was told that this was the man who had caught the outlaw—Marshal Bill Crabtree was a man of very few words at any time—however, he was plainly surprised at seeing a Negro.

'They tell me you're a preacher,' grunted Bill Crabtree, when he did eventually get round to acknowledging Caleb. 'If I was you I'd stick to preachin' an' leave bounty huntin' to them as knows. You'll be a mighty rich preacher now. Maybe you can buy your own church.'

'I've had better bounties,' replied Caleb.

'Have you?' said Crabtree, raising his eyebrows slightly. 'I don't know the name and I know most of the bounty hunters in this part of the world.'

'Then you'd better remember this one,' said Caleb. 'I've been around for a few years now and I intend being around a few more. Now, can I go and collect my money?'

'The Reverend Caleb Black,' muttered Crabtree. 'That should be easy enough to remember. Sure, you can tell the mayor it's OK—I hear they're offerin' five hundred apiece for them Jones boys. Are you goin' after 'em?'

'No,' replied Caleb. 'I think I've had enough of Bullhead.'

'Can't say as I blame you,' grunted Crabtree. 'Just remember not to go causin' no trouble in my territory. I don't like bounty hunters, but I suppose there ain't a lot I can do about 'em. You just keep within the law and everythin' will be all right. Take one step out of line an' I'll take great pleasure in dealin' with you, preacher or no preacher. Got that?'

'Loud and clear,' grinned Caleb.

Half an hour later, Caleb had collected his $5,500 and, with Sheriff McCready's agreement, had placed it in the safe in

233

his office for safe keeping. He would have left it in the bank but, in common with all banks, they did not open for business until ten o'clock in the morning and Caleb fully intended to be well on his way by that time.

Marshal Crabtree and his two deputies left town with their prisoners at four o'clock that evening to catch the return train due in at Kingston at 5.30. Frank Sullivan was obviously in pain, but he received very little sympathy from Crabtree or the deputies. His one brief comment to Caleb as he left was that he was likely to be dead before he ever came up for trial. Caleb had already formed the opinion that US Marshal Bill Crabtree was one marshal who believed in shooting first and asking questions later.

Deputy Sheriff Mick Bywater made a brief appearance in the saloon that evening, which seemed to be doing rather better trade than normal, due in the main to the presence of Caleb and anticipation that the preacher would be only too willing to share his sudden windfall. All except Mick Bywater were disappointed. Mick thanked Caleb for his help, saying that he had learned a lot from him.

One of the most disappointed people was the Reverend Peter Manston, whose attitude towards Caleb had miraculously changed on hearing the news of the reward. However, the old bigotry very quickly reasserted itself when Caleb refused a donation to the church.

Caleb returned to his room at the hotel and, just to be on the safe side in case anyone thought he had the money with him and had ideas of relieving him of it, he locked the door and the window and placed his guns where he could get at them. He need not have bothered, it seemed that everyone knew that he had placed the money in the sheriff's safe.

TEN

Caleb was outside the sheriffs office before dawn broke and had to wait a few minutes until McCready arrived. The sheriff appeared relieved to see the preacher and made it plain that he had had visions of someone breaking into his office and the safe, so much so that he had been forced to check on things at about two o'clock that morning. He lost no time in handing the money over to Caleb.

'Which way are you headed?' he asked.

'I promised the people of Pisa that I would go there,' Caleb grinned. 'It seems they have a need for someone like me. At least, that's what the woman who owns the store says.'

'And the rest will do exactly as they're

told,' laughed McCready. 'Annie Blincoe; she's related to almost everyone there. I've met her a few times. Quite a formidable woman.'

'She seemed very subdued when I was there,' said Caleb, 'but then she did have a knife at her throat.'

'She survived bein' scalped in the old days,' said McCready. 'Only thing was it wasn't the Indians who scalped her, it was a scalp hunter who didn't care where he got his scalps as long as he got paid. He made a mistake with her though; he should've finished her off. Two days after he'd scalped her he suddenly found himself without his balls. I don't know if he survived or not.'

'Well, it would seem that I have a couple of christenings and at least one wedding to perform,' said Caleb. 'What I don't understand is even if they don't have a regular minister surely they go into Greenwood on occasion, or even come here to Bullhead. All that could have been sorted out quite easily.'

'I don't think you understand the nature of these people,' said McCready. 'I don't suppose for one minute that any of them have been to Greenwood in years and as far as I can remember they have never been to Bullhead. They simply don't want to know about the outside world. There's another small town further north from them, called Redcliffe, and that's just about the only other place they have anything to do with. Most of Redcliffe are related to Annie in one way or another. Annie Blincoe has the only store in both towns. She brews her own beer and most distill their own whiskey. They seem to get along pretty well on their own. I'm surprised they wanted you, a preacher is just about the last person they needed I would have thought.'

'Well, she asked for me and since I don't have anything else to do or anywhere else to go, I might as well. It could be an experience.'

'In more ways than one,' smiled Mc-Cready. 'Just remember, the Jones brothers are up there somewhere and I don't suppose they'll hesitate to kill you.'

'I'll keep a watch for them,' assured Caleb. 'OK, Sheriff, I can't hang about talking. It's been nice meeting you, but I don't suppose you want to see me again. I'll be on my way.'

Sheriff McCready simply nodded and Caleb rode out of Bullhead just as dawn was breaking and the storeowners were beginning to remove their shutters. Most nodded briefly as Caleb rode past but a couple totally ignored him. He smiled and left the town to the yapping of a small dog.

Although he had not taken a lot of notice about how to reach the pass up Warren Ridge, Caleb found it easily enough and about three hours later he was passing through the gully where the Jones brothers had attempted their ambush and, without actually being conscious of the fact, he found himself looking for the brothers.

In normal circumstances, a reward of $500 on each youth would have been of great interest to Caleb, but this time, with $5,500 in his pocket, he did not feel the need to pursue them, added to which it was plain that neither Sheriff McCready nor Mayor Sanderson of Bullhead would really appreciate his involvement and he was never one to outstay his welcome. At the same time though, he was a realist and knew that if he did chance upon the Jones brothers he would undoubtedly take them back to Bullhead and claim the reward. However, he was certainly not going to go out of his way to find them.

By evening, Caleb had reached the same place amongst some trees where he, Wally Barns and Mick Bywater had spent the night and he opted to do the same. This time however, there was no need to hunt for food, Mrs Bracewell at the hotel had provided him with a goodly supply of good bread, cheese and two large, raw steaks and a supply of coffee beans. After sniffing at the steaks he decided that the best thing he could do was cook them both since he had serious doubts about the raw meat remaining edible for another twenty-four hours.

Dawn found him once again on the way to Pisa—or so he thought. Somewhere along the trail he realized that he must have taken a wrong turn or followed what he thought was the right track and was not. However he had done it, and now found himself in a stretch of forest which he had definitely not passed through before. The fact that at some points it was almost impossible to tell where the regular trail went probably explained his mistake. He remembered one particular stretch which crossed moorland with no clearly defined track. However and wherever he had taken the wrong trail was, at that moment, unimportant, the priority was to get himself back on the road to Pisa.

About four hours after setting off, he breathed a sigh of relief when he saw what appeared to be a homestead. It was one of the smallest he had ever seen, but there was no doubt that it was occupied as he caught a glimpse of a woman coming out of the door and emptying a bowl. There was also a thin plume of smoke issuing from the chimney. However, his approach to the cabin was anything but welcoming.

The shot echoed around and although he leapt from his horse and took cover, it was plain that the shot was intended to warn and not kill. It had not been a rifle shot but the duller thud of buckshot and, at the distance he was from the cabin, would never have reached him. Eventually he stood up warily, raised his arms slightly and called out.

'Hold your fire!' he shouted. 'I don't mean no harm. I'm lost and need help.'

'Just keep on ridin', mister!' came the

male voice in reply.

'My name is Caleb Black,' he called again. 'The Reverend Caleb Black ... ..

'Reveren'?' called the man again, suspiciously. 'What the hell brings a minister out here? There ain't nobody to preach to 'cept a few like us, some bears an' some wolves an' you probably got more chance of preachin' to the bears an' wolves than us. We don't like strangers here, we seen enough of 'em this past couple of days.'

'I'm not here to preach to anyone,' said Caleb. 'I'm coming up to the house. You just hold your fire, my guns are staying where they are.' He took the reins of his horse and slowly walked to the cabin, ensuring that the occupants could see that he was not attempting to go for his gun.

'That's close enough!' ordered the man. 'State your business an' maybe I'll listen or be on your way.'

'I'm lost,' said Caleb. 'I'm trying to reach Pisa. A woman named Annie Blincoe is expecting me.'

'Annie Blincoe?' queried the man. The door opened and a young man appeared, his shotgun aimed steadily. 'What business could you have with her?'

'You obviously know her,' replied Caleb.

'Ought to, she's my grandma,' replied the young man. 'That don't answer my question though. What business could you possibly have with her?'

'It would seem that she requires my services as Minister of Religion,' replied Caleb, taking couple of steps forward, to which the young man raised the gun, threateningly. 'Something about weddings and christenings.'

'How come you know Annie?' demanded the young man. Caleb sighed and explained briefly just how he had come to be in Pisa and even explained what the town and Annie Blincoe looked like. The young man lowered the gun and grunted. 'Sounds right enough,' he said. 'First time I ever heard of a preacher bein' a bounty hunter though. You sure you're a preacher?'

'I have papers to prove it,' replied Caleb.

'Papers don't prove nothin' as far as I'm concerned,' he laughed. 'I can't read or write.'

'Then you'll just have to take my word for it,' said Caleb. 'Now, could you please point me in the direction of Pisa?' The young man appeared to ignore this request.

'If'n you're a bounty hunter I reckon you should be goin' after two men who've suddenly appeared,' he said. 'They turned up here last night an' tried to steal my mule. They didn't succeed though an' I sent 'em off with some buckshot up their asses.'

'Aaron an' Jed Jones,' grinned Caleb. 'Maybe a bit younger'n you.'

'You know 'em?' said the young man. 'You sure it ain't them you is really after?'

'I know them,' Caleb confirmed, 'and no, it wasn't really them I was after. However, if I do get the chance I will

245

take them back to Bullhead and claim the reward which is out on them.'

'Then they can't be too far away,' said the young man. 'OK, mister, I believe you. Pisa is about two hours away at the most. You can't miss it, just keep followin' the trail an' take the right fork across a river about three miles up the road. Other fork leads to Redcliffe.'

For the first time, the woman he had seen earlier also appeared in the doorway, this time carrying a baby. She looked coyly at Caleb for a moment and cooed at the bundle in her arms.

'Annie sending for you could explain what she was talkin' about yesterday,' said the woman. 'My name's Martha an' this is my husban' Seth ...' She smiled self-consciously. 'Well, we ain't really man an wife, leastways we ain't had no churchin' marriage. Annie stopped by on her way to Redcliffe while Seth was out huntin' an' she said somethin' about gettin' me an' Seth churched proper an' the baby christened. We don't have us no regular preacher an' Annie allus takes advantage of one whenever she can, which ain't all that often.'

'We did have us a preacher who stayed for about six months,' Seth said. 'That was about two years ago but he soon got fed up an' left.'

'Then I hope to see you in Pisa,' smiled Caleb, raising his hat slightly. 'Just keep following the road, you say.'

'Take the right fork across the river,' reminded Seth. Caleb nodded his understanding, remounted his horse and without another word rode back to the trail. However, his mind was not really on finding his way back to Pisa. The news that the Jones brothers were in the vicinity suddenly interested him far more and from that point onwards his eyes and ears were on the alert.

Even with the news that they were in the vicinity, his initial reaction was not to actually go looking for them. However, he found, as he rode and considered things, that his previous determination not to look for them was rapidly beginning to wane, the thought of the $1,000 reward rearing its head.

He was within sight of the ford across the river when he saw them; at least he saw two figures suddenly run from the water's edge on the far side of the river into the forest behind them and from what he saw he was certain that it was Jed and Aaron Jones. His hands automatically went to both his guns just to loosen them slightly in their holsters, but he did not draw, preferring to give the impression that he had not seen them.

To have simply ridden on through the ford as though he was completely unaware of their presence would, he thought, have been the same as asking to commit suicide so, instead of crossing, he turned his horse off the trail on to a patch of grass on the nearside of the river, dismounted and pretended that he was resting. After a time he wandered casually amongst the trees, taking his rifle with him.

Once in the relative safety of the forest, he immediately crouched low and ran as fast as he could towards what appeared to be a series of rocks across the river, which in fact proved to be a small set of rapids, but since the water level was not too high, a crossing to the opposite bank was obviously quite easy. He did not cross immediately, waiting instead out of sight surveying the opposite bank.

He watched and waited for about ten minutes before he was satisfied that there was nobody watching for him and then crossed with an agility and speed that surprised even himself.

His crossing was not too soon. As he crouched amongst the trees, he saw, perhaps twenty yards up the bank towards the ford, the quite distinct figure of Aaron Jones also crouching and looking. Aaron appeared to make a signal and Caleb saw

Jed Jones suddenly dash across the ford, up a small bank and grab at his horse plainly intent on stealing it. He had a good view of the animal and Jed and both were within range of his rifle; he took careful aim and then remembered that the reward specified that the boys must be alive. He lowered his sight slightly and fired.

Jed seemed to spin round as the bullet slammed home and although he fell, apparently lifeless, Caleb knew that he was still very much alive. He had aimed for his hips and it was not very often that he missed his target. Immediately, Aaron Jones was running along the bank towards his brother, yelling at the top of his voice and plunging into the river just below the ford, which proved to be a deep pool. Caleb ran from the trees and then along the bank and waded into the ford, his rifle trained on Aaron who was puffing and wheezing his way to shallower water. He had not seen Caleb.

'I'd say that was the first bath you've had in years,' grinned Caleb, as Aaron suddenly looked up in horror.

'Bastard!' he managed to grate. 'You killed Jed.'

'I shouldn't think so,' smiled Caleb. 'He's goin' to have difficulty walkin' for a while, that's about all. Now, unless you want some of the same treatment, I suggest you come out of that water, drop your guns on the bank and do the same with Jed's.'

Aaron dripped out of the river, threw his Buchel rifle on to the bank and ran towards his brother who had an old Nutting rifle and an Adams revolver. Very foolishly, Aaron snatched at the revolver and twisted round to shoot at Caleb, although the shot was well wide. Even Caleb had to admit that he was taken by surprise and it was with a great deal of difficulty that he stopped himself from shooting to kill. Once again he lowered his aim slightly and his shot thudded into the top of Aaron's leg.

'That was a very stupid thing to do,' said Caleb. 'I could easily have killed you.'

'Why didn't you?' growled Aaron.

'There's five hundred reasons why not,' grinned Caleb. 'Dead, you're worth nothing, alive, you are worth five hundred dollars—each!'

'Five hundred ...!'

'Each,' emphasized Caleb. 'Nice of you to give yourselves up so easily. The town of Bullhead has seen fit to offer a reward of five hundred dollars each. Personally I wouldn't have offered more than fifty, but I don't mind, at least it makes it worth my while to take you back.'

By that time Jed was beginning to recover and eventually looked up into the black, grinning face of Caleb. He spat and swore, threatening to get even.

'I told him to leave you alone,' said Aaron, looking up at Caleb. 'We saw you comin' down the track an' Jed insisted that he was goin' to kill you an' take your horse an' guns. I told him to leave you alone.

I said it was bad luck to kill a preacher, even a black preacher, but he insisted.'

'You should have learned to move faster,' said Caleb. 'I saw you, that's why I pulled up where I did. Now, I reckon you can walk although it might be a mite painful but it looks like your brother will have to ride my horse. We are going back along the trail a while to a homestead—I believe you tried to steal a mule from there. I'll borrow their mule, maybe even buy it off them, and take you back to Bullhead. Mr McCready and the mayor will be pleased to see you even if they aren't very happy about seeing me.'

Seth Blincoe—he was related to Annie Blincoe through the male line—proved very co-operative and agreed to lend Caleb his mule, although the best he could do for a saddle was a couple of blankets. Martha cleaned the wounds but there was little else she could do other than roughly bandage them. Aaron and Jed spent the night trussed on the floor whilst Caleb slept on a rough bed above them. Seth and Martha occupied their usual bed at the opposite end of the room.

The following morning, Martha supplied them with some bread and cheese and Seth promised to walk into Pisa and explain to his grandmother the reason for the delay. At dawn, Caleb set off for Bullhead, which they reached the following morning. Once again the bush telegraph was ahead of their arrival and it was a hostile crowd which greeted them. At first, Caleb was uncertain if the hostility was aimed at him or the Joneses, but he eventually decided that it was aimed at the brothers.

'I thought you weren't interested in going after them?' grumbled Mayor Sanderson when Caleb confronted him in his office, demanding his money.

'I wasn't,' grinned Caleb, 'but if a thousand dollars just dropped into your lap would you refuse it?'

'I suppose not,' muttered the mayor.

'We've been thinking about that reward, perhaps we were too hasty in offering that much ...'

The gun was in Caleb's hand and the barrel being forced up one of the mayor's nostrils before he could blink.

'You were saying, Mr Mayor?' prompted Caleb.

'I ... er ... er,' gulped the mayor. 'I said that some members of the council thought that five hundred dollars each was a little too generous. I didn't agree with them and ... er ...' He glanced down at the gun still prodded into his nostril. 'It was eventually agreed that the amount be allowed to stand. I ... I'll see to it that your money is ready in half an hour.'

'That's just what I thought you said,' grinned Caleb, removing the offending gun. 'I'll meet you at the bank in half an hour.'

Sheriff McCready, although not too glad to see Caleb, was pleased to have the Joneses in custody, pointing out that at least it had saved him a lot of bother.

Deputy Mick Bywater, his head still bandaged, seemed to be the only person except Mrs Bracewell at the hotel, who was pleased to see Caleb.

With the news of a further $1,000 in his pocket, it suddenly seemed to hit Mrs Bracewell that, by her standards at least, Caleb was now a very rich, single and eminently eligible man, despite the colour of his skin and the knowledge that any relationship between a white woman and a black man was at the very least completely unacceptable socially and possibly even against the law.

The effect of her not-so-subtle advances was to make Caleb leave Bullhead that afternoon and not the following morning as he had intended. He could take most things life threw at him, but when it came to a woman, he would rather have taken his chances in a fist fight with a grizzly bear. He was not completely happy until, with the mule in tow, he had cleared the pass up Warren Ridge and was on his way to Pisa.